Mills

BEST SELLER ROMANCE

A chance to read and collect some of the best-loved novels from
Mills & Boon—the world's largest publisher of romantic fiction.

Every month, two titles by favourite Mills & Boon authors will
be republished in the *Best Seller Romance* series.

Rachel Lindsay

SECOND BEST WIFE

MILLS & BOON LIMITED
ETON HOUSE   18–24 PARADISE ROAD
RICHMOND   SURREY TW9 ISR

First published in Great Britain 1982
by Mills & Boon Limited

© Rachel Lindsay 1982

Australian copyright 1982
Philippine copyright 1982
Reprinted 1982
This edition 1988

ISBN 0 263 76064 2

Set in Monophoto Baskerville 10 on 11 pt
02–0488–57835

Printed and bound in Great Britain by
Collins, Glasgow

CHAPTER ONE

JULIA GOSFORD slipped the cover on to her typewriter and then swivelled her chair towards the window to look twenty floors down into the street. The traffic had already built up considerably and she knew if she were to leave now she would be caught in the thick of the rush hour. She turned back to her desk with a sigh, half wishing she had taken Adam Lester's advice and gone home when she had finished his personal mail. Yet she was always reluctant to leave the office early, in case he returned with more work.

Pushing back her chair, she stood up and stretched, stopping abruptly as the door swung open and Adam Lester came in. He was a tall, spare man with dark hair and eyes, broad of shoulder and exuding a commanding vitality that never left him no matter how tired he was. He was obviously very tired now, and he looked at Julia with such a blank expression that she knew instantly his thoughts were miles away. Well, not so many miles, she decided wryly, guessing they were with Erica Dukes, the woman who had held him enthralled for the past year.

It was a liaison Julia deplored, not only because the woman was the third wife of Kenneth Dukes, a self-made millionaire of gutsy character and brash behaviour, but because she was a hard and determined go-getter, who seemed to display little loyalty to anything other than money. Adam Lester could not help but know it, yet it apparently served as no warning to him. But then why should it? In every relationship he had had since Julia had started working for him, he had always been the one to walk away first. Yet with Erica Dukes it might be a different story. Julia gave herself a mental shake. What her employer did in his private life was no concern of hers. She was the three wise monkeys rolled into one: seeing, hearing and speaking no evil—though perhaps for the word evil, she should substitute mischief.

'Is anything the matter, Mr Lester?' she asked, her voice soft and melodious.

'What?' With an effort he focussed on her. 'Yes, there is. Mrs Dukes' husband died an hour ago, of a heart attack.'

'Oh dear.' It was a feeble response, but Julia could think of no other. 'He wasn't very young, was he?' she added after a pause. 'But I suppose it's always a shock when it happens.'

'Yes.' He frowned. 'Erica—Mrs Dukes—is completely alone. I can't see her stepchildren being any comfort to her.'

Julia hesitated, then curiosity overcame her discretion. 'Where did Mr Dukes die?' she asked slowly.

'At his house in the country. I've come back for some papers and I'm driving Mrs Dukes to Maidenhead this evening.'

'Will you be in tomorrow morning?'

'Of course. Why not?'

'I ... er ... I thought with the funeral ... the arrangements ...'

'It isn't my affair,' Adam Lester said coolly. 'His children are old enough to deal with it. My only concern is with Mrs Dukes.'

Who was definitely his affair, Julia added to herself, watching her employer stride into his office and dump a wadge of papers into his briefcase. Holding it under his arm, he came back into the outer office. He was still frowning, his brows lowered over his dark eyes, making their expression difficult to read.

'I promised Mrs Dukes I'd tell her friends what happened. But once I start on the phone, I'll never get off. It'll save me a hell of a lot of time if you'd do it for me.'

'Of course. Do you have a list?'

'No. But call all the people in my private address book—except my own family, of course.'

'I'll do it right away.'

With a nod of thanks he walked out.

Julia went into his office for his personal address book and then settled down to make the calls. It took more than an hour to contact everyone she thought necessary. Her employer had a large circle of friends—many of them also his business associates—and she had often wondered if he saw them socially because he liked their company, or because they were useful to his career. Yet he was now an international lawyer of world repute, and no longer required friends to bring him new clients, being kept so busy by multi-national corporations that his schedule was fully booked for the next eighteen months. But old habits tended to die hard, and Adam Lester was still inclined to socialise with the people he represented. This frequently meant late nights, entertaining or being entertained, and he would often come into the office heavy-eyed and short-tempered.

As she replaced the receiver after her last call, Julia could not help wondering what difference Kenneth Dukes' death could make to her employer's life. Would he marry the beautiful Erica or would she go on being his mistress? Somehow Julia could not see the marriage as a lasting success, but then she was prejudiced against the ice-cool blonde who always treated her with bare civility whenever she called Adam on the telephone or came—on rare occasions—to the office. Still, the one good thing that might come out of such a marriage was a lessening of his work load. With a wife at home, he would have less incentive to take legal briefs to bed.

With a faint smile Julia opened her desk drawer and took out her bag. She was meeting Roy at seven-thirty and unless she hurried she would be late. The thought of Roy filled her with warmth, and she marvelled that it

was only three months since they had met. In that short
time he had become such a permanent part of her life it
was difficult to remember what it had been like without
him. Realising it was too late for her to go home and
change, she hurried across the corridor to the cloakroom
to tidy. Roy hated to be kept waiting; something which
was guaranteed to put him in a bad mood for the rest of
the evening.

'You're much too conscientious,' he had said to her not
so long ago. 'I hope Mr Lester appreciates you.'

'I don't work hard to win appreciation,' she had
replied. 'I do it because it's necessary.'

Her calmness had quashed his irritability, but since
then she had made a point of being on time when they
had a date for the evening. It was strange that Roy should
object to her conscientiousness when he was exactly the
same. But perhaps he thought it was different for women.
To him they were creatures to be cherished and cosseted,
and he expected them, in turn, to treat him with equal
deference. It was the only subject on which they did not
see eye to eye, for Julia considered herself completely
emancipated. Indeed, she had reached the stage where
she was no longer even conscious of it, taking it for granted
that women had equal status with men. But Roy did not
accept this. They had had several arguments on the subject, and Julia had soon learned it was best to hold her
tongue, convinced that in time Roy would become less
dogmatic. She glanced at her watch and saw that it was
ten minutes past seven. Hurriedly she powdered her nose,
ran a comb through her thick auburn hair and headed
for the elevator.

She arrived at St James' Street with five minutes to
spare, and stood, as arranged, on the north corner watching out for Roy's car. Within moments she saw it coming
towards her, as pristine in appearance as its owner. Come
to think of it, she had never seen Roy casually dressed or
even the least bit untidy.

The car stopped and he leaned across and opened the door.

'You look happy,' he smiled, as she got in beside him. 'Been waiting long?'

'Only a minute.'

'Good.' Roy turned into St James' Street and headed towards an empty parking space. 'We can eat first if we hurry—unless you'd prefer to wait until after the show?'

'I'm easy. Afterwards, perhaps?'

'Are you sure you won't be hungry?'

She shook her head. 'I had some cake with my tea. I shouldn't have really. It's bad for the figure.'

Roy looked her up and down as he locked the car. 'There's nothing wrong with your figure, Julia. If anything, it's too perfect.'

'Too perfect?' She was puzzled, and showed it.

'It attracts men,' he said seriously, 'and I don't like it.'

'Oh, Roy,' Julia was delighted, 'don't tell me you're jealous!'

'You know I am.' His calm voice was unexpectedly jerky. 'If I had my way, I'd hide you beneath a black veil.'

'You're in the wrong country,' she teased. 'Women aren't in purdah here.'

'More's the pity.'

Roy caught her under the elbow and they began to walk. At five feet eight inches, he was only slightly taller than herself, and she never wore high heels when she went out with him. Roy liked to feel he was a big man, a conceit to which she pandered. Height apart, she found him good-looking, though in an understated way, with pale skin that flushed easily, light brown eyes and sleekly brushed hair of the same colour. At their first meeting she had assumed him to be a lawyer or an accountant, and since he was an actuary, she had not been far out.

'I've had an excellent day,' he said, breaking into her

thoughts. 'Mr Phillips was very complimentary about my report on the Calgary Oil boom.'

'Does that mean he may offer you the job in Canada?'

'He already has—this morning.'

'Roy!' Julia stopped walking and looked him fully in the face. 'Why didn't you tell me?'

'I'm doing it now.'

'I mean right away, when you first saw me?'

'Actually I was keeping it to tell you at dinner.'

Julia felt her cheeks grow pink, wondering whether Roy had planned, at the same time, to ask her to marry him. The thought frightened her—surprisingly so, since she had been dreaming about it for the past month.

'Mr Phillips wants me to leave immediately,' Roy continued.

'What do you mean by immediately?'

'As soon as I get clearance from Canada House. That should be some time next week.'

'Next week? But how can you go so soon? Don't you have things to clear up here?'

'Nothing that can't be done by the man who takes over from me.' Roy had resumed walking and Julia kept pace with him. 'Practically everything's arranged,' he added. 'I've even got one of the chaps in the office to take over the lease of my flat, and he's willing to buy all the contents too. I'll have the use of the company flat in Toronto until I decide exactly where I want to live, so there won't be any problems. It's merely a question of getting things organised.'

'You're very good at that,' Julia said automatically, mulling his words over in her mind and trying to find some hint that he intended asking her to go with him. But if he did, surely he wouldn't expect her to leave at a week's notice? 'I'd never be able to clear things up as fast as you,' she added.

'That's because you're a woman.' A smile softened his comment. 'They're hoarders by nature, and want to take everything with them. If you were in my shoes, it would probably take you months to get ready.'

'Not months,' she corrected. 'But certainly several weeks. Still, the question doesn't arise, does it?' she said lightly. 'I can't see myself moving anywhere in the near future.'

This time it was Roy who stopped, and his grip on her arm tightened. 'I have to get settled first, Julia. It will be an entirely new life for me, even though it's with the same company. But I'll be working with a new boss, a foreigner, and I have to feel my way.'

'Canadians aren't foreigners.'

'To me they are. But once I'm settled, I shall want a home and a wife. You know what I'm trying to say, don't you?'

'I think so. But I'd like you to actually say it.'

He smiled faintly. 'I love you, Julia. I thought I'd made it pretty obvious.'

'Not all that obvious,' she smiled back.

'What more could I have done? I've seen you three times a week for the past three months,' he said, as if quoting statistics. 'You're not the sort of girl I envisaged marrying, but . . .' He coloured as he saw her surprised expression. 'What I mean is that you're too beautiful. I know it's hard for you to understand this, but I dislike being made to feel jealous of you. And I am. Extremely jealous.'

'I'm glad,' Julia said softly, and leaned towards him.

He caught her hand and squeezed it tightly. 'As soon as I've settled in Toronto, I'll arrange for you to come out.'

'What for?'

'What for?' He was astonished. 'To marry me, of course.'

'You haven't asked me yet, Roy.'

'Oh, darling, I'm sorry.' He was contrite. 'How stupid I am! Will you please marry me?'

'Most definitely,' Julia smiled, and ignoring a group of

approaching people, moved close against him, hoping he would kiss her. But he only gave her a brief hug before pushing her away. Then thinking better of it, he put an arm around her slender waist and kissed her hard on the mouth. Julia instantly clasped his shoulders, wanting his kiss to deepen, but Roy drew back.

'Not here, Julia. What will people think?'

'I couldn't care less,' she laughed. 'It's not every day I get a proposal of marriage. Oh, Roy, stop being so inhibited!'

'I can't help it. That's the way I am. I'm a solemn stick, Julia, and I can't change. If you have any doubts——'

'Don't be silly,' she interrupted. 'I know we don't agree on lots of things, but as long as we have the same basic principles, our differences won't matter.'

'I hope not,' Roy said solemnly. 'There'll be certain adjustments you'll have to make, but if you're willing, there shouldn't be any problems.'

Julia was curious as to what sort of adjustments he meant, but they had reached the cinema and she had no chance to ask him. Yet the question remained with her, making it difficult for her to concentrate on the film. How inconsequential fiction was compared with the reality of her own life! What would it be like to be married to Roy? She wouldn't have the adventurous life she had always hoped for; it would be a far more serious affair—possibly even mundane. Oh, heavens, she thought guiltily, why am I thinking this way? What did it matter if Roy was a little too serious and conservative? At least he would never be unfaithful to her. Once he had pledged his loyalty to a wife, he would forsake all other women.

And that was the most important thing for her to know. Acknowledging this, Julia realised how deeply she had been affected by her parents' marriage. As a child, she had assumed them to be happy. But later she had realised that her father, who had been exceptionally handsome and charming, had been totally incapable of remaining faithful to any woman; adding this to his extravagant tastes and inaptitude for work, one had a recipe for a deeply unhappy marriage. By the time Julia was sixteen, her father had left and returned home at least half a dozen times, and with each departure and reconciliation, Julia's mother had aged more. Only in the last years of his life had Jack Gosford stopped roving, a situation brought on more by failing health than any change of character. Even so, his death in a car accident when Julia was twenty had so shattered his wife that she had died three months later.

Because of her father, Julia had vowed to steer clear of fickle charmers, determined that the man of her choice would be, above all, reliable. And Roy indisputably was. Stability was the one characteristic which had most attracted her to him. Of course his pomposity could be irritating at times, but this was nothing compared with fecklessness and infidelity.

Later that evening, when he kissed her goodnight outside her flat, Roy held her with a firmness that delighted her, displaying a passion that took her by surprise.

'You won't go out with anyone else while I'm away, will you?' he demanded. 'Promise me, Julia.'

'Do you have to ask?' she said reproachfully. 'I wouldn't put that sort of question to *you*.'

'Because you know it isn't necessary. But you're so beautiful. A man only has to look at you to want you.'

'You talk as if I'm some kind of temptress,' she said.

'You are, but it's something you can't help.'

Although flattered by his comment, Julia found it disquieting. She had never given Roy cause for anxiety, and wondered if it stemmed from something deeper than jealousy. He wanted her, yet he seemed ashamed of his desire: that was why he resented her beauty.

'It's your colouring and your figure,' he went on. 'You attract attention, Julia, even though you don't want to do it.'

'Then don't blame me for it.'

'I'm not. I just wish you wouldn't wear make-up, and could change your hairstyle.'

'Would you like me to wear glasses and a veil?'

Realising he had said the wrong thing, Roy flushed unhappily. 'I'm sorry, dear. I'm talking like a fool.'

'Like a man in love, rather,' Julia said quietly, regretting her sarcasm. 'Love me as I am, Roy. The *me* that's inside the glossy package.'

'That's what I want to do,' he said thickly, and started kissing her again.

Julia parted her lips, her heartbeats quickening. But even as she began to deepen the kiss, he drew back, his body stiff with tension.

'No, Julia,' he said quickly. 'Don't touch me.'

'Why not? Oh, Roy, come into the flat and kiss me properly. It's not every night a girl gets engaged.'

'If I come in with you, I may not be able to leave.'

'I might not ask you to,' she whispered.

'No,' he said firmly. 'I respect you too much. I want us to wait till we're married. Otherwise I'd feel it was wrong.'

'That's usually a woman's line,' Julia smiled, accepting his reluctance and reminding herself that Roy hated to show his emotions, and must find his life quite different from the ordered existence of three months ago. Still, he had asked her to marry him, so he must be ready for change. Or was he hoping to change *her*?

Remembering his remarks about her appearance, she felt a vague sense of apprehension. Did he really find her auburn hair too colourful and her figure too perfect? It seemed so ludicrous she could not believe he had meant it seriously. It was definitely jealousy that had made him say it; once they were married, he would learn that despite her looks, she was loyal and faithful.

CHAPTER TWO

ADAM LESTER drew the car into the kerb and switched off the engine. But he did not immediately get out. Instead, he rested his hands on the wheel and stared at the windscreen. It was a fortnight since he had seen Erica, and then it had only been a brief glimpse at her husband's funeral, where they had had no chance to talk. That same day, an important case had unexpectedly sent him halfway across the world to Aden, keeping him there until last night, when he had returned home too late and too tired to do anything except climb into bed.

While away, he had rung Erica several times, and on each occasion had become more convinced something was wrong. But she had been evasive when he had asked her, and he was too wise to insist, accepting that she would not disclose anything until they saw each other. He wondered if it was connected with Kenneth Dukes' will, and whether he had finally shown resentment of her infidelity. Yet somehow Adam doubted it. Kenneth Dukes had stopped being a husband in the true sense of the word long before he himself had come on the scene, and had made it plain he did not mind how many affairs his young wife had, as long as she remained discreet. Surely he had not gone back on his word and shown his displeasure by leaving everything to his children? But what matter if he had? Adam shrugged. Erica would want for nothing once she became his wife. Still, women were strange creatures, and Erica strangest of all. She might not like being punished from the grave.

Slipping the ignition key into his pocket, Adam walked up the flight of marble steps into the spacious foyer of a luxurious apartment house. The Dukes had moved here a few years ago, when Kenneth started to spend more time at his home in Maidenhead, leaving Erica the run of the penthouse, which had suited her admirably.

When Adam stepped out of the private elevator directly into the penthouse lobby and saw Erica coming towards him, his heart beat as fast as a schoolboy's on a first date. It was not that she was particularly good-looking—he had seen women far more beautiful—but none seemed to have her special blend of fire and ice; a mixture he found exhilarating. Her milk-white skin contrasted with her full red mouth; her pale blonde hair was a foil for passionate dark eyes, while her slender, almost too thin body was redeemed from boyishness by high, full breasts.

She was very much a creature of contradiction; not only physically, but mentally too: one moment aloof, the next, clinging; one moment commanding, the next submissive.

At the moment she appeared cool and controlled, though she kissed Adam warmly and rested for an instant in his arms, before leading the way into the living-room which overlooked a wide, flower-filled terrace.

'You don't look a bit tired after your trip,' she commented, moving to the drinks tray and returning to hand him a whisky and soda.

'Sheik Achmad believes in early nights,' he smiled, 'and the social life in Aden isn't exactly to my taste.'

'I'm glad to hear it.'

'Don't tell me you're jealous?'

'I've never been jealous of any man.' Dark eyes glowed mischievously. 'I suppose you think that's conceited?'

'Realistic, rather!'

Erica chuckled, then stopped, convincing Adam that something was worrying her.

'Tell me what's wrong,' he said softly. 'I guessed there was trouble when I spoke to you on the telephone. Is it something to do with Kenneth?'

'I'm afraid so.' She perched on the arm of a settee, her full-skirted dress of black chiffon floating gracefully around her. 'Kenneth was a very clever man, you know. That was one of the reasons why I married him. His being a millionaire was only part of his attraction.'

'You needn't sell Kenneth to me,' Adam said dryly. 'He was a client of mine long before he married you. And all this talk of cleverness . . . What are you leading up to? Has he cut you out of his will?'

'The exact opposite. I would have been able to cope with *that*. But he's done something far shrewder. After extremely generous bequests to his children, he's left everything to me—on condition that I don't remarry for four years.'

Adam was too well trained a lawyer to show his astonishment. 'I suppose it would be naïve of me to enquire whether the will is valid?'

'One hundred per cent valid,' she rejoined. 'I stand no chance of contesting it.' She jumped up and glided across the room, her delicate white hands clasped together. 'It would have been better if he'd left me nothing. I'd have been upset and angry, but I'd have got over it.'

'I should damn well think so,' Adam said forcefully. 'As my wife you won't be short of anything.'

'But to leave me most of his estate and then tie it up in this way,' she went on, speaking as though she had not heard him. 'That's where he's been so Machiavellian.'

'I grant you it's a neat trick, but there's no need to get het-up about it. You won't be exactly poor, married to me.'

'But three million pounds!' Erica muttered. 'I can't just turn it down.'

Adam sipped his whisky and tried to hide the deep anger that Kenneth's action had aroused. The man was clever all right. Machiavellian was exactly the word to describe the way he had managed to use his death to come between Erica and himself.

'Why is Kenneth's money so important to you?' he asked quietly. 'I'm not in his league financially, but I'm perfectly able to keep you in the fashion you want.'

'I know that. But three million is a great deal to walk away from. Think what we could do with it.'

'We?'

'Of course. Once we're married, whatever I have will be yours. We only have to wait four years, and then we'll be able to buy a country house, and an apartment in New York—look how many times you go there on business. Why, you could even give up law if you wish and concentrate on the stock market. I'm sure you could double our assets if you did.'

'I've no intention of giving up law, nor will I wait four years to marry you.' Adam set down his glass with a bang, his resolve to keep his temper forgotten. 'This past year has been bad enough, without four more like it.'

'But it wouldn't be the same. We had to be discreet for obvious reasons, but with Kenneth dead, we can live together openly. It wouldn't matter.'

'It would to me.'

Erica looked startled. 'Do you mean that? In these emancipated days?'

'Damn right I do! I'm not merely a lawyer by profession—I believe in upholding it too. Marriage may be regarded as outmoded in some circles, but in my opinion it's a fundamental bulwark against declining ethical standards.'

'Only moral ones, surely?' Erica questioned.

'No, ethical ones too. Man's attitude to marriage is also part of his social structure—and the social structure is linked with the ethical and moral one.' Aware of sounding hectoring, Adam softened his voice. 'I want more than a casual relationship with you, Erica. I want a lasting foundation to my life. Living together may be fine for youngsters and showbiz people, but it's not for me.'

'It wouldn't be a permanent thing, darling,' Erica pleaded. 'Only until I've complied with Kenneth's crazy rule. Once the four years are up, we can be married. A ring on my finger and a legal bit of paper won't make me feel more your wife than I already do. Please be reasonable about it. It would be madness to turn our back on all that money.'

'What you're really saying is that you want the best of both worlds.' Adam moved away from Erica, knowing it was imperative for him not to be swayed by the potent physical power she had over him. 'I won't let Kenneth rule our lives for the next four years. I love you and I want to marry you *now*. There's also the matter of children. I'm thirty-five and I have no intention of waiting till I'm forty before I become a father.'

'We don't have to wait,' she said.

Adam marvelled that Erica, who had always been so careful to keep her good name and social standing intact, should have no such worries when it came to having his illegitimate children. But then wasn't three million pounds a strong incentive to alter one's attitudes? Except that it wasn't altering his own. He frowned, not liking where his thoughts were taking him, yet too intelligent to ignore them.

'No,' he said slowly. 'I want my children born in wedlock.'

'You seem to set more value on your unborn children than you do on loving me!'

'That's a foolish comment,' he retorted. 'If anyone should question the meaning of the word "love", it should be me. Tell me, Erica, how much is my love worth to *you*? Not three million pounds, that's for sure, if you're willing to forgo marriage because of it.'

'Forgo?' Erica echoed, her eyes dilating. 'When did I say I wouldn't marry you? All I'm asking is that we delay it.'

'I don't want to delay it.' Roughly he stepped forward and pulled her tightly against him, his desire surging at the feel of her slender body. 'Doesn't it mean anything that I desperately want you for my wife? That I want to proclaim to the world that we're together?'

'We can still do that,' she whispered. 'To all intents and purposes, I'll still be your wife. Be reasonable, darling.'

'Reasonable? Damn it! I'll feel like a kept man. Everyone will know you've put your greed for Kenneth's money before your desire to be my wife.'

'I wish you wouldn't talk in such a melodramatic and old-fashioned way,' Erica cried, pushing him away from her. 'What you're asking me to do isn't the suggestion of a man who loves me, but of a selfish egotist who can't bear to wait until he's made me into his possession. Think of the position from *my* point of view. If I'm willing to live with you openly, doesn't it show I trust you?'

'Oh, sure,' he replied. 'But it also shows I take second place to your late husband's money.'

Bright colour flushed Erica's pale skin. Instantly it spoiled the patrician fineness of her features, making her look hard and ugly. But as the colour faded, the delicacy returned to her face and her dark glowing eyes filled with tears.

'I didn't realise you could be so cruel, Adam. You talk as though I don't love you, when all I want is to increase our security.'

'My security is strong enough not to require another man's fortune,' Adam said harshly as he strode to the door. He was halfway through it when Erica ran across and barred his way.

'You can't go!' she cried. 'We love each other.'

'*I* love *you*,' he corrected. 'But you love money.'

'I'm being realistic,' she repeated. 'But you're being chauvinist, as well as proud.'

'I won't deny either accusation,' he said. 'But I happen to want a wife and a mother for my children.' He gently pushed her out of his way and crossed the hall to the elevator.

'I'll be waiting for you,' Erica called. 'You're the only

man I want, and I won't settle for anyone else.'

Adam did not answer, but her words echoed in his ears as he went down to the main floor and out to his car.

The whole of the next week Adam buried himself in his work, determined not to call Erica. If he did, it would only lead to his agreeing to her terms, and he knew that if he succumbed in a moment of weakness, he would live to regret it. Yet his need of her increased until it was an ache in his heart and a surging throb in his loins that no work could dispel. His resolve to stay away from her was weakening, and he searched desperately for a prop to give him strength.

Fortuitously, at the beginning of the following week he received a call from a colleague attached to the International Court at the Hague, which necessitated his having to fly to Holland to help settle a difficult case. He was in a calmer frame of mind by the time he returned to London at the end of the week, and was as determined as ever to remain true to the principles which had parted him from the woman he loved.

He was sitting at his desk, wondering what to do with himself during the weekend—any more work and he would become mentally stale—when the private line on his bedside table rang. Instinct told him it was Erica, and he experienced a swift urge not to take the call, afraid that if he heard her voice, it would weaken his resolve.

And it did. Her husky tones brought back memories of the passionate hours they had shared, and when she tearfully said she wanted to see him, he was so overcome by her unusual breakdown of control that he instantly agreed.

'I'll call for you at eight-thirty,' he said. 'I'll book a table somewhere quiet.'

'Why not dine with me here?' she suggested.

'I'd prefer not,' he lied, knowing that if he did, they would end up in the bedroom.

'Very well, then.' There was a purr in her voice which

told him that she knew why he had refused. 'I'll wait for you downstairs, Adam—far be it from me to tempt you.'

Erica was waiting in the lobby when his car drew up at the kerb. As soon as she saw him she came gracefully down the steps. She had taken special care with her appearance, he noticed, and was wearing one of his favourite dresses: a silvery grey silk that made her hair seem more ash than blonde, and gave her the appearance of a silver reed. Except that there was nothing reedlike in her unbending will. He had always known that once she took a stance she would stand by it, and he had been pleased that, despite her fragile appearance, she was a woman of strength. But that was before she had used her strength against him—as she was doing now.

Yet he was strong too, and he had no intention of giving in to her demands and living with her. What the hell did she take him for? A callow youth happy to wag along behind her like a puppy dog, waiting till she had complied with her late husband's wishes and could inherit all his money? No, it was not on. If she loved him she would marry him at once. He had a beautiful home in London, adequately staffed and more than enough money in the bank. He also had a brilliant career and an even more brilliant future. But this didn't seem to be enough for Erica. She wanted gilt on the gingerbread. He smiled sourly. Perhaps it was more accurate to say she wanted gold on it.

He took her to dine at Les Ambassadeurs, instead of one of their usual frequented quieter places in Soho. But then they no longer had to be discreet about their relationship.

'Have you missed me?' she asked, raising her glass of wine and staring at him across the rim of it.

'Do you need to be told?'

'A woman always likes to be told.'

'I missed you every moment of every day, and I still want to marry you—as soon as possible.'

A shadow crossed her lovely face. 'I was hoping you'd changed your mind,' she said beguilingly. 'We shouldn't waste these four years, Adam.'

'That's how I see it too. Which is why I want to marry you.'

'You're still being old-fashioned,' she said petulantly.

'And you're still being mercenary.'

Her mouth narrowed, making him conscious that half of its fullness came from the skilful application of lipstick.

'That's a beastly thing to say to me!' she cried.

'But the truth. I meant every word I said the last time we met, and though I've missed you like hell, I haven't changed my mind.'

'Nor have I. So where does that leave us?'

'It leaves you looking forward to a big bank account. As for me . . .'

'Yes?' she asked. 'And where does it leave you?'

'On the lookout for another woman.' He saw the disbelief in her eyes and it spurred him to say angrily: 'I mean it, Erica. If you intend waiting for Kenneth's money, then I'll marry someone else.'

'Just like that!'

'Just like that.' He glanced around the room, the tilt of his dark head arrogant, then acknowledged the greeting of a man and woman at a table some few yards from theirs. Erica's eyes followed his and she stiffened.

'You can't be thinking of Angela,' she said angrily. 'She likes horses more than men.'

'She's never given me that impression,' Adam replied. 'But no, I wasn't thinking of Angela.'

'Who else, then? For the last year you haven't looked at anyone other than me.'

'And I'll be happy not to look at anyone else if you marry me, but if you don't . . .'

'I want to go home,' Erica said abruptly. 'And I don't want to see you again until you've come to your senses. Your attitude to Kenneth's money is unrealistic and I've no intention of arguing with you any more. There's only one thing I have to say, and that is that no matter what you believe, you'll never be able to forget me easily.'

'I never said it would be easy,' Adam replied, escorting her out of the restaurant. 'But I intend to make a life for myself either with or without you.'

Erica did not answer, nor did she speak again until he went round to open the car door for her outside her apartment block.

'So this is goodbye,' she whispered, her brilliant dark eyes lustred with tears.

'So it would seem.'

'Even though I love you and want to be yours?' Her slender hand caressed his cheek. 'Think of me when you're lying alone in bed at night, Adam. Remember my touch and the feel of my body.'

'You hit below the belt, don't you?'

'I want you, and I'm trying to make you realise how much you want me.'

'Oh, I realise it all right, but I'm going to fight it.'

'It's a battle you'll lose, Adam, but I promise I'll make the defeat very wonderful for you.'

Without looking back she went into the foyer, and Adam returned to the car and drove away, accepting that the next few weeks of his life were going to be the hardest he had ever faced.

Once again he immersed himself in his work to the point where he became so overtired that his temper was frequently at flashpoint. He knew his staff were finding him impossible, but it was not until Miss Gosford, whom he regarded as the perfect secretary, suddenly flung her notebook on the floor and walked out of his room that he realised he had to take himself in hand.

'Forgive my outburst,' he apologised, going into her office. 'I know I've been bloody to work for recently, but I promise to go away and relax this weekend—which should, I hope, improve my temper.'

'I should be used to your temper by now,' Miss Gosford replied, giving him the faintest of smiles. 'It's just that today I—I had some bad news, and things rather got on top of me.'

'I see. Is there anything I can do to help?'

'No, there isn't, thank you.' She bent over her type-writer, and realising she did not want to talk about her personal affairs, Adam returned to his room and picked up the papers he was working on. Within a moment all else was forgotten.

True to his word, he flew to Scotland for a golfing weekend. He played six solitary rounds, tired himself into exhaustion and returned on Monday feeling considerably more relaxed.

It was an attitude that began to fade when he dis-covered Miss Gosford was away with a migraine.

'I didn't know she suffered from that,' he said sharply to Miss Smith, the girl who had temporarily taken her place. 'When will she be back?'

'She said tomorrow.' Miss Smith hesitated. 'Personally, I think she should stay home a few more days. She really wasn't at all well. Perhaps you could suggest it to her?'

'Just over a headache?'

'It's more than that.'

'What do you mean?'

'Well ... she's been jilted.' The girl looked embarras-sed. 'But please don't say anything to her until she tells you.'

'I never intrude into my staff's personal affairs,' Adam said coldly.

'I know that. But Miss Gosford has been your secretary for three years, and I assumed you knew she was going to be married.'

'Married? I had no idea.' Adam stared down at his desk, feeling somewhat ashamed. 'Miss Gosford is so effi-cient I tend to forget she's a person with feelings. I'm saying it as a compliment,' he added quickly, looking up to see the girl's frown. 'But now you've told me what's wrong, I'm quite happy for her to stay away for the rest of the week.' He pointed to the telephone. 'Get her for me, will you?'

His secretary's voice sounded jerky and indistinct when she came on the line, and Adam suspected she had been crying.

'Miss Gosford?' he said. 'Adam Lester here.'

'I'm sorry I wasn't in the office today,' she said quickly. 'I hope Miss Smith is managing? I'll be back tomorrow.'

'Miss Smith is managing excellently, which is why I'm calling you. I want you to take a few days off. It will do you good.'

'It's very kind of you to suggest it, Mr Lester, but I'd rather not. I'm sure I'll be well enough to come in tomorrow.'

Adam hesitated, knowing that work was the best panacea against heartache. 'Very well, then. I'll see you in the morning.' Replacing the receiver, he looked at Miss Smith. 'Miss Gosford's coming in,' he said. 'It's probably better for her than sitting at home moping.'

Remembering Miss Smith's comments about his secretary, Adam watched Julia Gosford with unaccustomed awareness as she entered the office next day. She was paler than usual, and this made her hair more noticeable. The colour of burgundy wine, he thought. And very striking too.

He rose with a smile. 'I hope you're feeling better, Miss Gosford?'

'Yes, thank you, Mr Lester.'

She sat down in front of him and crossed her legs. They were long and slim and he noticed how slender she appeared in a narrow tailored skirt and blue silk blouse. Julia Gosford was a tall girl who held herself well; her shoulders were straight and her head was erect, though now it was slightly tilted, enabling him to see the smooth line of her creamy neck, where her hair lay coiled in a loose bun. It was an unusual style for a young woman; he vaguely recalled it as belonging to the flapper era. But no one could call Miss Gosford a flapper; she was much too staid.

'I'm glad you're back,' he said sincerely. 'I would find you extremely difficult to replace.'

'No secretary is indispensable.'

'*You* are.'

She blushed, the colour accentuating the creamy texture of her skin. He was irritated with himself for noticing it—he never had before—and assumed it was because he knew that, like him, she had been let down in love. There was nothing better than fellow suffering to give one a sense of camaraderie.

'I hope I'll be with you for many years yet, Mr Lester,' she went on.

'Unless you leave me to marry?' Adam said deliberately, his face devoid of expression.

'That's very far from my mind.'

'Selfishly, I'm glad to hear it, though I find it hard to believe no man has yet discovered you.'

'There *was* someone,' she murmured, 'but he—he went to settle in Canada and fell in love with someone more suitable.'

'More suitable? I don't follow you.' Adam was, surprisingly, curious. Perhaps his recent hurt over Erica was making him more sensitive to other people's problems.

'It's ridiculous really,' she murmured, 'but Roy always said he found me too—too attractive, and he couldn't bear other men to look at me.'

'You're joking?'

'Oh no. He said it made him feel insecure.'

'It sounds as though you're well rid of him, Miss Gosford.'

'You're probably right,' she replied. 'Though at the moment I'm too hurt to see it that way.'

She bent her head to her notebook, indicating that she

was ready to take dictation, but Adam was reluctant to start work. What would his secretary say if he told her about Erica and her reasons for not wanting to marry him? Would she agree with Erica or would she feel the world well lost for love? Yet he had no intention of asking her, and was amazed he was even interested in what she might think. It was Miss Smith who had made him suddenly aware of Miss Gosford as a person, instead of an efficient machine in his office, catering to his business needs.

Frowning, he picked up a document and was about to start dictating when the telephone rang. Miss Gosford lifted the receiver, spoke a few words and then passed it across to him, mouthing the words 'Mr Burglass'.

'Hello, Jack,' Adam said brightly. 'I was going to call you later.'

'I'm not calling on business,' Jack Burglass replied. 'I've been given some tickets for Covent Garden for tonight— *La Bohème*. I know you like opera and I wondered if you and Erica would care to join us?'

'I'd be delighted, personally speaking, but I'm not sure what Erica's doing.'

'How come? I thought you always knew what she was doing. Anyway, when's the wedding? Or is that being old-fashioned?'

'Very old-fashioned,' Adam replied smoothly.

There was a momentary silence before Jack Burglass spoke again.

'Sorry if I've got my wires crossed, old chap, but I did have the feeling you were serious about her.'

'I'm always serious about my current girl-friends,' Adam said coolly. 'Do you mind if I cut the call short, Jack? I have a client waiting.'

'Oh sure. But what about the opera tonight?'

'May I bring someone else along if Erica can't make it?'

'Naturally. We'll meet in the Crush Bar half an hour before the curtain goes up.'

Adam put down the receiver and frowned. Who the hell would be free to go out at such short notice? He picked up his address book. He had not looked at it since meeting Erica, and he was certain all his previous girl-friends were long since out of circulation. He wondered if he should call Jack and tell him he could not make it tonight after all. Yet to do so smacked of defeat, and he was not one to acknowledge such a thing without putting up a fight. He frowned again, not liking the fact that he was putting his emotional life into business terms. Erica was his love, his only love, and he found it hard to accept that she did not have the same intensity of feeling towards him.

'Should I come back later?'

With a start he realised his secretary was still waiting to take dictation, and he nodded. She rose from the chair and he watched her walk to the door. From the back, she seemed even taller, and he wondered if she found it a handicap. But surely not. What was it she had said to him a moment ago about beauty being a problem? It seemed nonsense to him. As if any man would object to a woman being too beautiful!

'Miss Gosford,' he called abruptly, 'would you be free to come to the opera with me tonight?'

Only as she swung round and he saw the surprise on her face did he realise how unexpected she found his in-vitation. Dammit, he found it unexpected too, and he wished he hadn't asked her. But it was too late now.

'If you're busy,' he went on, 'then forget it. It was merely a thought.'

'I'm not busy tonight, Mr Lester,' she said calmly, 'and I'd be delighted to go with you.' She hesitated. 'Are you going for business reasons?'

'Does there have to be a business reason for everything I do?' he asked testily.

'No, but——'

'I'll collect you at six-thirty, then. Please leave me your address.'

She looked discomfited. 'It's miles from where you live, Mr Lester. It would be much easier for you if we met at the theatre.'

'But not easier for *you*,' he replied. 'I'll arrange for Parsons to pick you up and bring you to my home.'

With a nod, she went out, and Adam leaned back in his chair. His regret at having proffered the invitation was beginning to recede, particularly when he thought how astonished Jack would be at seeing him with someone other than Erica. Though he had told him he might bring someone else, he was pretty sure Jack didn't believe him. All at once, Adam's ill humour vanished. By this time tomorrow, Erica would know he had been out with another woman. Beryl Burglass was the worst possible gossip, and she'd start broadcasting it first thing in the morning.

Well pleased by the thought, Adam picked up his pen and concentrated on the document in front of him, though it was still several moments before his attention was sufficiently caught for him to stop thinking of pale blonde hair and a tantalisingly passionate mouth.

CHAPTER THREE

JULIA did not normally have to think what to wear, but that evening she changed her mind twice before deciding on a simple black dress. The dark colour was a perfect foil for her pale skin, and gave her hair the sheen of ruby velvet. On her way home she had called at a chemist and bought some make-up, defiantly choosing items she had never used before: grey-blue shadow to draw attention to the deep blue of her slanting eyes; mascara to darken her long lashes, and flame red lipstick to outline the sensual curve of her mouth.

Her hair remained her most noticeable feature and, still in a mood of defiance, she loosened it from its coil and let it ripple down to her shoulders. How Roy would have cringed! Adam Lester would be surprised too, but he deserved it; expecting to see the sober, decorously clad young woman he had employed for over three years, he would find himself confronted by a Technicolor beauty. A beauty? She eyed herself in the mirror. Well, she was, and there was no longer any reason to pretend otherwise; not now that Roy had shown her how foolish pretence had been.

It had started with her father. From the moment she had realised how easy it was for a beautiful woman to attract her father's attentions, Julia had been afraid her own striking looks would draw the same kind of faithless man; hence her determination to play down her appearance to the point where it had almost become a disguise. Even so, quite a few men had sensed her potential—after all, it had not been possible to hide her height nor the graceful proportions of her slender body—but only Roy, with his serious-minded sincerity, had made her drop a little of her guard. And how wrong she had been. Within days of arriving in Canada, he had fallen for a pert little blonde and written a contrite letter asking Julia to release him from their engagement.

In doing so, Julia had also released herself, though it had taken Adam Lester's invitation to the opera to make her fully aware of it. Come the weekend, she would go shopping for a new wardrobe to match her new way of thinking. Of course her dislike of men remained as strong as ever, but from now on she would dazzle them all and remain heartwhole, giving away nothing of her innermost self.

She was waiting on the front steps when George Parsons, Adam Lester's chauffeur, arrived to collect her. He pressed the bell of her flat without realising she was standing beside him, and only as she gave him a smile did he return it with a dazed look of recognition. However, he was too discreet to comment, though he smiled warmly when she opted to take her place beside him in the front.

'That's what Mr Lester always does,' he said. 'Unless he has work to do. Then he sits in the back.'

Unwilling to discuss their mutual employer, Julia smiled and said nothing, though the chauffeur's comment made her wonder what she was expected to call her employer that evening. It would seem odd if she addressed him as Mr Lester, yet she could not call him Adam unless he asked her.

As they drove past Hyde Park Corner and drew nearer to his home, her thoughts turned to the unexpectedness of tonight's invitation. It was quite clear Mr Lester had stopped seeing Erica Dukes. She had suspected it when the woman's telephone calls had ceased coming through on his private line, and had been positive when he flung himself into his work with even more fury than usual. But was the estrangement permanent or the result of a lovers' quarrel that would soon run its course? Devoutly Julia hoped it was the former, and that Adam Lester would find someone less selfish than the beautiful blonde. It was obvious that his invitation to herself had been the result of pique; of anger that a man in his position should be caught without a girl to escort. It was a rare occurrence for him, and one not likely to happen once he put his mind to finding someone else.

With these thoughts uppermost, Julia arrived at his elegant Chester Street home. It was the first time she had been there, and she was impressed by the marble entrance hall and the charmingly furnished drawing room into which the butler led her. It was surprisingly informal, due in the main to the preponderance of photographs and flowers that stood on the many small tables dotted around the rug-strewn floor. A log fire beamed in the large grate, though most of the warmth came from the slim radiators half hidden by softly billowing apricot curtains.

Her employer rose as she entered. His dark dinner jacket made him seem taller and more saturnine, though his smile of welcome was warm. However, he did not come forward to greet her, but stood watching as she moved across the room towards him. The centre light tuned her hair into a blaze of colour which was echoed in the black and wine red shawl she had draped over one arm, the ends of which trailed on to the carpet. Julia knew, from the gleam in Adam Lester's eyes, that he liked what he saw. Faintly irritated by the condescending way he waited for her to approach him, she stopped abruptly.

'Do I meet with your approval, Mr Lester?'

'Most certainly, and the name is Adam.' His look was slow and deliberate. 'Were it not for the colour of your hair, Miss Gosford, I'd never have guessed it was you. I should think that every man who sees you tonight, will envy me, and unlike your erstwhile fiancé, I shall be delighted to show you off.'

'Please don't mention Roy,' Julia said stiffly.

'Why not? Don't you still think of him?'

'Of course.'

'Then why be afraid to talk of him? It's the best way to get him out of your system.'

'If you say so, Mr Lester.'

Adam's mouth tightened, then relaxed as he smiled. 'You're not as docile as I thought, Julia.'

'I'm not in the office now.'

'That's not the only difference. You don't look the same person either—as you're only too well aware. But tell me, which is the real you? The businesslike woman with the bun and colourless demeanour, or the glamorous creature in front of me tonight?'

'Do I have to be one or the other?' she countered. 'Can't I be both?'

'I'm not sure if the two are compatible.'

Nor was Julia, but she was loath to admit it.

'What happens tomorrow?' he asked. 'Which female will I be seeing in the office?'

'The same one you're seeing tonight.'

'Does that mean you've turned over a new leaf?'

She gave his question some thought. 'It means I've stopped raking over the leaves of someone else's past,' she admitted, burying her mother's unhappiness alongside her own anger against Roy. 'From now on, I am as I am.'

Adam Lester raised an eyebrow. 'We should drink to that, I think, except that we're pushed for time. We'd better delay it until we get to the theatre.'

Sitting beside him in the back of the car, Julia realised she had never before been so close to her employer. It increased her perception of him, making her conscious of his height and the breadth of his shoulders. Nor had she noticed until now how thick and silky his hair was, and the compact way it lay against the nape of his neck. Relaxed though he appeared to be, she felt the tension that lay within him: like a coiled spring that might unwind too fast and go snap. He shifted his position slightly, the better to look at her, and a wave of expensive after-shave lotion prickled her nostrils.

She drew back in her seat, warning herself not to read too much into this evening. Still smarting as she was from the blow Roy had dealt her pride, it would be all too easy to rebound into somebody else's arms; and it would be the height of foolishness for those arms to belong to the man beside her. Adam Lester had invited her out because she had been the most convenient girl to come into his mind when Jack Burglass had invited him to the opera. As a date of his own choosing, she would never have been asked.

'If anyone wants to know what I do,' she ventured, 'should I tell them I'm your secretary?'

'I'd object if you said you were anyone else's,' he answered. 'I'm no snob, Julia. You should know that by now.'

'But you've never taken out any of the girls who work for you.'

'I never knew I had such beauty right under my nose.'

'Don't!' she said sharply. 'It isn't necessary for you to put on an act until we're with your friends. You know very well—and so do I—that I wouldn't be here with you tonight if . . . if . . .'

'I take your point,' Adam Lester intervened quietly, 'and I apologise. You're too intelligent to fool, and I should have known better.'

Her reply was forestalled by their arrival at the Opera House. The downstairs foyer was packed with people, though it was as nothing compared with the aptly named Crush Bar.

'Is it always like this?' Julia demanded breathlessly, as they squeezed their way up the shallow, carpeted stairs.

'Usually, and always when it's a gala night—like tonight.'

'Adam!' Jack Burglass was upon them, rotund and beaming. He gave Julia a swiftly appraising look, but there was no recognition in it, and she hid a smile.

'You've already met Julia,' Adam said easily.

'Not me, old chap,' Jack Burglass replied promptly. 'I never forget a beautiful face.'

'You've forgotten this one, I'm afraid.' Adam put his hand on Julia's arm. 'It was in my office, the other day: behind a notebook and pencil.'

'Behind a . . .' Jack gaped and peered closer. 'Good lord! Miss Gosford. I didn't recognise you. You look completely different.'

'That's not very complimentary,' Adam grinned.

Jack looked at him reproachfully before smiling at Julia. 'I can see why you don't come to the office dressed like this. If you did, no man would get any work done!'

'I'd have found it a bit of a problem, I must say,' Adam put in, placing a hand possessively on Julia's arm and drawing her slightly in to his side.

Julia allowed him to hold her, marvelling that he could put on such an act; for act it definitely was. He should have warned me, she thought irritably, and edged away from him. Jack Burglass noticed it and smiled slyly, and with increasing annoyance Julia knew she had done exactly as Adam had wanted. By playing hard to get, she was making it all too clear why Adam was on the prowl.

'Come over to the bar,' their host said. 'I've some bubbly on ice.'

The bar itself was even more crowded than the room around it, and with some difficulty they squeezed their way to the far corner.

'Erica's here,' Jack murmured to Adam, over his shoulder. 'Have you seen her?'

'No. Not for a few days. I'll try to have a word with her during the interval.' Adam looked and sounded unperturbed. 'I haven't seen much of her since Kenneth's death.'

They reached the corner, where Jack's wife Betty, and an American couple, were waiting for them. The Americans, who were both lawyers, were soon engrossed in conversation with Adam, leaving Jack and his wife to talk to Julia.

'Do you find Adam easy to work for?' Betty Burglass asked. 'I bet he can be quite a tyrant at times.'

'Only when you don't do as he wants,' Julia smiled. 'But he's trained me well. I've been with him nearly four years, so I know how to cope with all his moods.'

'Why can't you keep *your* secretaries that long?' Betty asked her husband.

'I'm not as good-looking as Adam!' he chuckled.

Julia was glad when the warning bell rang and they could make their way to their box. She looked around the theatre for a glimpse of Erica, and but even as she espied a pale bonde head, the house lights dimmed and the overture began. From then on, Julia was transported into a magical world, where poverty led to love, and love to exquisite music and song. Roy and his shallow loyalty seemed a million miles away, though the hurt he had caused her returned with painful force when the lights went up at the interval. Quickly she glanced at Adam, her sadness forgotten as she saw it mirrored upon his own face.

'Don't look like that,' she murmured impulsively. 'No person is worth it.'

'That doesn't ease the pain,' he said, leading her out of the box to the Crush Bar.

He appeared to have changed his mind about speaking to Erica, and remained beside Julia for the entire interval, talking to her with an intensity which the rest of the party noticed. Once again she was irritated by his assumption that she would play along with him, but compassion for him made her do it; aided by the romantic music she had just heard and the champagne she was drinking.

It was after one o'clock when Adam finally dropped her outside her home, having dismissed Parsons once he had met them with the car outside the Opera House.

'It's been a wonderful evening for me,' she said. 'I'm glad you invited me.'

'It was Jack's evening really,' he smiled. 'But perhaps next time you'll let it be mine?'

'Will there *be* a next time, Mr Lester?'

'Mr Lester?' he echoed. 'What's happened to Adam?'

'It's after midnight,' Julia replied, 'and I'm changing back to Cinderella.' Suddenly recollecting how that story had ended, she said hastily: 'What I mean is that the play has ended and we're returning to the status quo.'

'Hardly,' he said with a faint smile. 'Julia of the long red hair can never go back to being the prim Miss Gosford. Anyway, I thought you were giving up that disguise?'

'I'm getting cold feet.'

'Then plunge right in,' he ordered. 'It's the only way.'

Julia watched him run down the steps to his car, and only when he had driven away did she close her front door. What an unpredictable man he was: combining warmth with aloofness; hardheadedness with sentimentality, though admittedly the sentimentality was rarely shown.

As she prepared for bed, she wondered why she had continued working for him for so long. He was not the easiest of employers and she had received many other offers—quite a few from his clients who, impressed by her efficiency, would have paid her considerably more than she was getting. But she had turned them all down without thought, and only at this moment did she find herself wondering why. She supposed it was because working for Adam was exhilarating. He gave all his cases a sense of urgency which prevented one's interest from flagging. And he was also appreciative when you used your initiative and things went well, rewarding you not only with a bonus, but with the time he took to tell you personally how well he liked what you had done.

Slipping on her nightdress, Julia snuggled between the sheets. She was as wide awake as a cricket, and knew that sleep was a long way away. Curiosity to know the reason for Adam's estrangement from Erica Dukes stirred her imagination, for his attachment to the woman had lasted longer than any of the others she could remember in all the years she had worked for him. When she had first become his secretary, he had changed girl-friends as frequently as she herself changed shorthand notebooks, and every single female in the office had done her best to catch his eye. But to, no avail; the one rule Adam Lester never broke was to mix business with pleasure.

Until tonight, that was. Julia pulled a face. Not that Adam's evening with her had been all that much of a pleasure for him, regardless of how charmingly he had pretended it was. He had taken her out in order for it to get back to the lovely Erica, and it would be as well to remember it. She cast her mind back to Erica's entry into her employer's life. Kenneth Dukes had been his client for many years and, until two years ago, had been a frequent visitor to the office. Then his health had declined and he had spent most of his time in the country, since when Adam had started to see Erica.

It had begun as a mild flirtation, and Julia had been given the task of buying flowers for him to send to her. This soon changed, and he started to choose the flowers himself—a sure sign of his deepening interest. But now it seemed as though the affair was over, and Julia wondered if it was because Erica had expected Adam to marry her when her husband had died, and he had refused. Yet if this were the case, why was he depressed? Could his unhappiness be due to the fact that he wanted to carry on living with Erica as before, but that she wouldn't agree? The more Julia thought about it, the more puzzling it became, and she decided that though she knew a great deal about her employer's working life, she was completely mystified when it came to his emotional one.

Entering the office next morning, she felt slightly embarrassed. But Adam's greeting was so natural that she soon lost her shyness, and within moments was taking dic-

tation in her usual efficient manner, once more the perfect
secretary.

'Do the letters right away,' he concluded, leaning back
in his chair and looking at her. 'And as soon as I've signed
them, have them delivered by hand.'

'They should be ready in an hour.'

He nodded, and Julia went out, feeling vaguely let
down. She had been waiting to hear if he would call her
Julia or Miss Gosford, and had ruefully noticed that he
had carefully avoided using either, which still left her in a
state of uncertainty.

She returned with the letters within the hour, as
promised. Adam was finishing a telephone conversation,
and she knew from his tone that he was speaking to Erica
Dukes. As he put down the receiver and took the folder
from her, she was even more certain of it, for his face was
flushed and looked angry. Quickly he scrawled his signa-
ture and handed her back the folder.

'When you've given the letters to Parsons, come back
in here,' he said abruptly. 'I want to talk to you.'

Julia nodded and, having found the chauffeur, returned
to Adam Lester's room. He was still at his desk, and looked
in no better frame of mind. The lovely widow certainly
had it in her power to anger him.

'Take a chair,' he said abruptly, 'and put away your
notebook.'

Julia complied, then waited for him to speak. But he
remained silent, staring into space, as if he had forgotten
that anyone was in the room with him. He really was
good-looking, she thought, eyeing him dispassionately,
and with his charm and intelligence, was capable of
breaking many hearts.

'I've something to ask you, Julia.' Adam Lester finally
spoke, the sharpness of his tone startling. 'It's about . . .'
He paused, biting his lower lip with his strong white teeth,
and frowning deeply, as if all the cares of the world had
been thrust upon his shoulders. 'It concerns Mrs Dukes,'

he went on. 'I've just been speaking to her, and she told me that the newspapers have discovered the terms of her husband's will.'

'That doesn't surprise you, does it?' Julia commented. 'I mean, they were bound to ferret it out. After all, Mr Dukes was very rich and used to enjoy publicity when he was younger. He must have known the papers would try to create a last story around him.'

'Yes . . . well, you're probably right. I daresay he did know—and was looking forward to it.' Again Adam paused, his anger replaced by embarrassment, which sat oddly on his saturnine face. 'I'd better tell you the whole story, since it happens to be connected with something else I wish to say.' He twirled a gold pen between his long, slim fingers. 'Dukes left his wife the bulk of his fortune on condition that she does not remarry for four years. If she does, she loses the lot.'

'Good heavens!' Julia had never liked Erica, but this act from the grave seemed unnecessarily cruel. 'Did Mrs Dukes have any idea he was contemplating such a thing?'

'No, definitely not. Their marriage ceased to mean anything to either of them years ago, but they remained excellent friends. He also made a point of telling her— and his children too—that he didn't want them to mourn him. He said he'd had a good innings and he wanted his family to enjoy the rest of their lives.'

'He seems to have changed his mind as far as his wife is concerned,' Julia murmured, and was convinced this was the reason for Adam Lester's unhappiness. *He* had wanted marriage; after years of playing the field he had finally succumbed—the only pity being that it was to such an unworthy subject. But the subject, unhappily for him, was unwilling to forgo her husband's fortune.

'I was hoping to marry Mrs Dukes,' Adam said quietly. 'But—well, now you know why I shan't.'

'She turned you down because of the money?' Julia asked boldly.

'Yes. It was a lot to expect her to give up.'

'But you're not exactly on the breadline!'

'Compared with Dukes' millions, I am,' Adam said abruptly, and fell silent again.

'Why are you telling me all this, Mr Lester?' Julia asked, using his surname deliberately.

He did not answer.

'There must be a reason,' she persisted.

'Yes, there is.' Adam slid his chair towards the window. The sun poured straight down on to his head, making his hair gleam like jet, though the light made it difficult for Julia to read his expression.

'Since Kenneth Dukes' death,' he continued, 'all my friends have been expecting us to announce our engagement. When the details of Dukes' will become known— plus the fact of Erica not agreeing to marry me—you can imagine what a fool I'll look.'

'I don't see why. Quite a few of your friends will think she's being very intelligent about it.'

'Because she shows she loves her late husband's money more¹than she loves me? I'm not a pauper, for God's sake! Certainly I've more than enough money to keep a woman happy, no matter how extravagant her tastes.'

Since the woman he loved had made it unmistakably clear that she did not happen to agree with him, Julia saw silence as being the best kind of diplomacy.

'I know what you're thinking,' he said flatly, 'so don't just sit there like a dummy!'

Annoyed, Julia spoke. 'Do you want me to say I think Mrs Dukes is behaving despicably?'

'If that's what you think, then yes.'

'Well, I do think it,' Julia retorted, still stung by his attitude. 'And I also think you were blind not to have seen what she was like months ago. You may be a sensational judge of character in your professional life, Mr Lester, but in your personal one you're a disaster!'

A wry expression crossed Adam's face. 'You don't pull your punches, do you?'

'It must be something I learned from you.'

'I'm glad of it. Because at least now I can be equally blunt.' His pause was momentary: only enough to draw a deep breath. 'I don't like being made to look a fool—and as you've rightly said, that's exactly what I've been. But I can still remedy the position—if you'll help me.'

'I'll do anything I can. You know that.'

'Even to marrying me?'

Julia's eyes widened and she found it impossible to speak.

'Marry me,' Adam reiterated. 'If you are my wife, everyone will think Erica was merely another of my girl-friends—no more important than any of the others.'

Still Julia was too stunned to reply. Had this idea been in the back of Adam Lester's mind when he had invited her to the opera last night, or had it only occurred to him after this last telephone call from Erica Dukes? But when-ever he had thought of it, to do as he asked was out of the question.

'Well?' he said. 'You're not usually at a loss for words.'

'I am now,' she muttered. 'And a good thing, too. Otherwise I might say something I'd regret.'

'Why are you so angry? What's wrong with my propo-sal?'

'What's wrong with it? Good heavens! I'm not a robot who'll do exactly as the great Adam Lester commands. Marriage isn't a business contract to *me*, and——'

'I'm sorry you feel insulted,' he cut in, though he did not look in the least sorry, merely surprised. 'Be sensible, Julia. Surely you can see my proposal has many merits. After all, you've also been disappointed in love, so you can't pretend you're starry-eyed about it. Or are you still waiting for Mr Right to come along?'

His question reminded Julia of the agony she had endured over Roy, and she shook her head emphatically.

'Well then,' Adam continued, 'what's wrong with a businesslike marriage? I think it has as much chance of succeeding—probably even more—than many that are entered into when blinded by passion.'

Julia could not deny this, and as her anger cooled she began to understand the reason for Adam's proposal, and to see some merit in it. Being Mrs Adam Lester had much to commend it from a material point of view—except that she wasn't sufficiently materialistic to consider it from this angle. Of course it also had merit on another plane too; for physically he was a strikingly handsome man who knew how to make a woman feel wanted.

Angry at where her thoughts were taking her, Julia frowned. The proposal was outlandish and she should turn it down out of hand.

'Mrs Dukes might still change her mind,' she said quietly. 'You'd be furious if you then found yourself tied to somebody else.'

'I've no intention of waiting for her to have second thoughts—which is exactly what my friends will expect.'

'So you think that if you marry someone else they'll realise you weren't in love with Mrs Dukes?'

'Not if I marry *any* woman,' he said, 'only *you*.' Adam slid his chair towards his desk so that he could rest his elbows on it. His jacket was unbuttoned to reveal his expensive blue silk shirt, the material of which rippled to show the muscles on his chest. 'If I were to marry you, everyone will think we kept our relationship secret to avoid gossip in the office. It would also explain why I let my name be linked with another woman.'

'Mrs Dukes being the cover, instead of the other way around?'

'It makes sense, don't you think?'

'Only up to a point. I mean, if you'd really loved me, you'd have married me before.'

'Perhaps I wasn't ready to commit myself. There are any number of reasons why I'd want to keep our affair under wraps until we'd both decided exactly what we wanted to do, and Erica was a wonderful way of doing it.'

'Even to the extent of going to bed with her?' Julia asked flatly.

'These days, men aren't faithful until they've actually decided on marriage.'

'And not even then,' Julia retorted. 'Your friends will really think I'm a first class idiot to be your part-time girl-friend and let you wander away whenever the fancy took you.'

'I don't see why. As I've just said, neither of us was totally sure, and until we were, we played it the modern way.'

'As you're so modern,' said Julia, 'why are you insisting on marriage? With Mrs Dukes, I mean.'

'Because I won't live with a woman for four years and take second place to her first husband's money. I'm also thirty-five, Julia. I want children while I'm still young enough to enjoy them.'

It was the first time Julia had heard Adam talk of children, yet it did not surprise her that he wanted his own. A man so concerned with his public image would wish to have children to carry on his name.

'You should at least marry someone who loves *you*,' she said firmly, 'even if you don't love *her*. I mean, if you expect to have children . . .' Embarrassed, she stood up. 'Your proposal is out of the question.'

'Are you hoping to be reconciled with your ex-fiancé, then?'

'I wouldn't have him back if he begged me. A man who lets you down once . . .' Julia stopped, unwilling to reveal her inner feelings to anyone, least of all this man, who treated marriage like a business contract.

'Then why be in such a hurry to turn me down?' Adam Lester asked quietly. 'It seems we've both learned a painful lesson. I personally have no intention of allowing myself to be hurt again, and I have the impression you feel the same way.'

'I do,' Julia said fervently.

'Mind you, I'm forgetting how young you are,' he went on. 'And you may very well change your mind if you meet some other man. Maybe you do still believe in love.'

'The more I believe in it, the more I'll fight against it,' said Julia. 'Love makes you too vulnerable, too open to hurt. I thought Roy was different, but he turned out to be no better than my——' she stopped short. 'No,' she continued huskily, 'I'm as cynical about the opposite sex as you are.'

'Then marry me.'

'But you want children,' she burst out, 'and I . . . No, it's out of the question.'

'Do you find me repugnant?'

Their eyes met and Julia reddened. 'No, I don't. But I . . .'

'I won't rush you,' he interposed. 'I'm willing to wait until we know each other better.'

'How long is better?'

'That will be for *you* to decide. Three months, probably. That should be time enough for you to have grown used to me. Say yes, Julia. I promise you our marriage will have a better chance of succeeding than most. After all, we've worked together for four years, and you've seen the worst side of me, haven't you? Don't they say a man is an open book to his valet and secretary? And of course, you know my friends and business acquaintances, and I'm sure you'll run my home as capably as you do the office.'

'You mean as second best, I'll do fine,' she said sarcastically.

'Won't I do fine as second best for you?' he countered.

Julia stared into Adam's face, comparing his decisive features with Roy's fine-cut ones. There was nothing delicate about Adam's strong nose or firm mouth with its full lower lip, any more than there was anything weak in the thick black eyebrows above the intelligent, glinting eyes.

'As my wife, you would want for nothing,' he went on, coming round the side of his desk towards her. 'You will have a lovely home, a generous allowance to do with as you will, and we'd have a marriage based on friendship and respect. What could be more civilised?'

Adam made it sound so simple that it seemed the height of stupidity not to concede. Yet it was his question about whether she was waiting for Roy to return that prompted her to nod her head. It was a slight gesture, but he saw it at once, and smiled.

'Good,' he said. 'You won't go back on your word, will you?'

'No, but——'

'I'll arrange for us to be married right away.'

'Why the rush?' she asked, suddenly afraid.

'Why do you think?'

'You're scared that Mrs Dukes will get around you?'

'Possibly.'

'I thought you were too tough for that.'

'So did I,' he sighed. 'But love makes fools of us all.'

'Not of me,' Julia stated. 'At least, not any more.'

They were words she was to remember later.

CHAPTER FOUR

FEARING Julia might change her mind, Adam announced their engagement in *The Times* two days later. The news caused a sensation among his friends, as well as in the office, and Julia knew that had she foreseen the furore, she would never have agreed to his proposal. Typically, Adam also chose the day of the announcement to go to Paris to see a client, leaving Julia to cope alone.

'I don't know how you managed to keep it so secret,' Susan Smith said to her. 'You could at least have given me a hint.'

'And become a continual source of gossip?' Julia grinned. 'Adam would have loathed it.'

'But no one even guessed! It's incredible. I still don't know how you managed to keep it a secret.' Susan eyed her enviously. 'Tell me, when's the great day?'

'I'm not sure.' Julia spoke without thinking, but seeing Susan's surprise, added hastily: 'I'm leaving it for Adam to decide.'

'I bet you'll have to leave everything to him. Is he as bossy in his private life as he is in the office?'

'I refuse to answer that,' said Julia, forcing a laugh, then stopped short as Adam entered the room. She hadn't expected him back from Paris till later in the day, and was unexpectedly pleased to see him. Without any hesitation he walked across and lightly kissed her on the cheek.

'Good morning, my dear,' he said, and held open the door of his room for her to precede him in.

Silently she did as he bid, and he swiftly closed the door and gave her an ironic smile.

'That went quite smoothly,' he commented. 'I don't

think Miss Smith suspects anything, does she?'

'Let's say she's suspended her disbelief,' Julia replied. 'But the whole office is awash with rumours of how I managed to snare you, and yesterday, when you conveniently absented yourself, the phones never stopped ringing.'

'There was no point in us both suffering,' he said with shameless honesty.

'I'll make sure it's *your* turn next time!'

'Fair enough. That's what our marriage should be, don't you think?—a partnership.'

'I can't see it becoming one,' Julia stated. 'You're used to being the boss—as you are here—and I doubt if you could change.'

'Don't confuse my professional self with the person I'll be at home,' he told her.

'You mean you're a Jekyll and Hyde?'

'Wait and see,' he smiled. 'Which reminds me, we needn't wait too long. The sooner we're married the better. If you're free tonight, perhaps you'll have dinner with me and we can discuss it?'

'As we've just got engaged, I'm not likely to be going out with anyone else.'

'How true,' he said, humour edging his voice. 'I merely asked out of politeness. I was always taught never to take a woman for granted!'

'Even your secretary?'

'You're my fiancée,' he corrected. 'And soon to be my wife.'

'I still can't believe it,' she said nervously. 'Are you sure we're doing the right thing?'

'We're doing the logical thing,' he answered, his expression serious. 'And since we've both eschewed romantic love, logic is all that's left to us.' He set his briefcase upon his desk. 'We'll have dinner at my house tonight, Julia. It's less public.'

'Shall I go home and change first, or leave with you?'

'Leave with me, of course. You look perfectly fine as you are.'

So much for fancy clothes, Julia thought wryly, knowing how dull her navy skirt and white blouse was by comparison with the dress she had worn at Covent Garden. She was wearing her hair in its usual coil too, pinned tightly upon the back of her head; not that Adam had noticed this either. But then why should he? She wasn't the woman he loved; merely the logical choice of a man who had decided to take second best.

The door behind them opened and Adam swung round. His features hardened visibly and Julia had no need to look round herself to know who it was who had come in unannounced. With commendable calm she turned. Erica Dukes stood on the threshold. Dressed in mourning lilac— black was only for aged or weeping widows—she looked the picture of brave sadness. Only her eyes denied the portrayal: icy cold and hard, they swept over Julia with contempt before coming to rest on the man.

'I want to talk to you, Adam,' she said softly. 'Alone.'

'You may talk freely in front of Julia,' he replied. 'We have no secrets from one another.'

'I think I could come up with one or two,' Erica replied, 'or does Miss Gosford know *all* your little idiosyncrasies?'

Faint colour tinged Adam's face, and he gave Julia a quick look which, ever the perfect secretary, she correctly interpreted by silently retreating into her own office. She was surprised to find she was trembling with anger, and pondered on whether it was against Erica for coming here, Adam for not standing his ground and sending her packing, or herself for caring what the hell he did. Little idiosyncrasies indeed!

With an effort Julia forced herself to do some work, but it was hard going, for she was on the alert for Adam's call. Did the advent of Erica mean he might change his mind about going ahead with his planned marriage? Considering she had her own doubts about its advisability, she could not understand why the idea of his backing out of it should be so disturbing. Of course if he did, it would mean loss of face for her, and also the necessity of finding another job; a discarded fiancée could not remain *in situ* once she had been replaced; and this alone was enough to make her despondent. With renewed effort she continued typing, and was on her third letter when the door of Adam's office burst open and Erica stormed past her, banging the door of Julia's room with such force that some papers lifted and fell to the floor.

'I'm sorry about that,' said Adam from the doorway of his room. Although his voice was calm, he looked distinctly pale, which accentuated the black of his hair and the thickness of his eyebrows. The scene with Erica had obviously upset him, and Julia guessed what it must have cost him to send her away. Suddenly she knew it was out of the question for her to go on with this pretence.

'Adam, I don't——'

'Julia, I——'

They spoke simultaneously, and stopped simultaneously too.

'Please go on,' Julia said automatically.

'I only wanted to say I think we should get married next Saturday. It's going to be embarrassing having you in the office, and there's no earthly reason for us to delay things.'

'I thought we were going to discuss the date to-night?'

'We were. But seeing Erica . . .'

Adam's voice was thin and Julia felt desperately sorry for him. Yet his misery was of his own making; caused by pride alone, which would not allow him to remain with the woman he loved, unless she proved that love in the way *he* wanted.

'If you weren't so obstinate,' she said, 'you could remain with Mrs Dukes.'

'We've already gone into the reasons why I won't,' he

replied, 'so for God's sake let the matter drop! Just tell me whether next Saturday suits you.'

As she stared into his eyes, bleak and pain-filled, Julia's doubts dissolved. If marrying her would help him recover his usual verve and strength, how could she refuse? As he had said only a short while ago, it was the logical thing for both of them to do.

'Saturday will be fine,' she answered.

'Good. Now clear out your desk and tell one of the other girls to take over from you. Miss Smith will probably be able to manage until I can get someone better.'

'Miss Smith will get better once she stops being petrified of you,' Julia informed him. 'Just be a little patient with her.'

'And say please and thank you?' he enquired sarcastically.

'That's fine for starters!'

Unexpectedly, he laughed. 'Oh, Julia, I'm beginning to realise how little I've known you in all the years you've worked for me. And here I was, thinking I was taking myself a meek little wife!'

'A meek little wife would bore you to death,' Julia said without expression, trying not to let him see how pleased she was that she could, even temporarily, bring a smile to his face. 'You need someone to argue with you and bring you down to earth from time to time.'

Dark eyebrows lifted. 'I thought I was always down to earth? It's what my clients pay me to be.'

'Down to earth in terms of your illustrious clients is different from the way most people think of it. A month in a Sheik's palace, and you return to the office and make life hell for everyone!'

'My, my, I *am* learning things about myself! Being married to you, Julia, is going to be like wearing a hair shirt!'

'You can always take it off.'

His eyebrows rose higher. 'You mean divorce?'

'Well, we're getting married in a register office.'

'It's legal and binding, nonetheless. And since I'm a lawyer, that's how I regard all contracts.'

'You may fall in love with someone else,' she ventured.

'So may you.'

'No.' Julia's blue eyes darkened like azure skies in a storm. 'I'm not looking for love, Adam. Quite the opposite. But if it does happen, then I shall tell you and ask for my freedom.'

'Good,' he said crisply. 'I promise to do the same. Now hurry up and clean out your desk.'

Julia felt sad at leaving the firm. Yet she agreed with Adam that it was far better for her to leave at once. In the years she had worked here, she had learned a lot. She had even, on occasion, thought of studying law: going to evening classes in the hope of qualifying as a solicitor herself. Now the idea would have to be abandoned, for she could not imagine Adam wanting his wife to be a career woman. In that sense he was like Roy. Yet not quite, for Roy had also disliked it when she had shown herself to be more knowledgeable on a subject than he was, whereas Adam enjoyed the occasional astute comments she made about one or other of his cases or clients and, even when disagreeing with her, had always taken the time to explain why he did. Perhaps she should ask him outright how he felt about her furthering her education.

The opportunity came that night, when she dined at his home. He had shown her over it briefly and then introduced her to the middle-aged couple who ran it for him, with the help of a younger Filipino woman.

'I can see I won't have much housework or cooking to occupy me,' she commented as she sipped the delicious artichoke soup. 'Would you object very much if I elected to study for a degree?'

'Not if you have the time and the inclination. But if we start a family, you won't have much spare time for a few years. I meant what I said about wanting children, Julia.'

She knew her cheeks were reddening but could do nothing to stop it. 'I realise that,' she mumbled. 'But I—I told you I couldn't live with you physically until I . . . until I got to know you better.'

'Can you think of a better way of getting to know me than by sharing my bed?'

'You know what I mean,' she protested.

'I'm not sure I do. We've known each other nearly four years, Julia; long enough for us not to be strangers with each other.'

'There's a difference between being business colleagues and being lovers,' she protested. 'Anyway, you promised to give me time.'

'I won't go back on my word. But I'm thinking in terms of months, not years. I want to be young enough to enjoy my children.'

'They'll be children of a woman you don't love,' Julia warned him, experiencing an odd pang of hurt as she said the words.

'They'll be the children of someone whom I admire and respect,' he countered. 'That's as good a basis as love—sometimes better—for love can blind you to many other important things.' He paused. 'As my love for Erica did.'

'Learning how to see was very painful for you,' Julia said softly, knowing how much Adam had always trusted his judgment.

'Yes, it was. But it's a lesson I hope I've learned well. No other woman will ever be able to blind me again.'

'How can you be certain? You make everything sound so cut and dried. Doesn't it ever worry you that things may not turn out the way you anticipate? That they could go wrong?'

'They already have,' Adam replied tersely, 'but see the good that's come out of it all? You, for a start.'

'A substitute only.'

'Is that how you see *me*?'

'You're not anything like Roy,' Julia replied quickly. 'You've a much stronger personality. Just as your Erica is more dynamic than I am.'

'Never *my* Erica.' Adam put his glass on the table with such force that wine splashed out, and Julia was surprised the stem did not break.

But no one could have been calmer than Adam on the morning of their wedding. And later, at the reception at Claridges, he gave the impression that he could not be happier. Julia decided that the stage had lost a great actor when he took up law, and wished she found it as easy to simulate. But each time Adam led her to a group of his friends, she felt herself stiffen awkwardly, and she was shaking with nerves when they cut the wedding cake and he kissed her full on the mouth.

Yet for all his bonhomie, he guessed her feelings, for he gave her hand a comforting squeeze. 'It's nearly over, Julia,' he whispered. 'In half an hour we'll be on our way to the airport.'

'I can't believe we'll be away for a whole month,' she whispered back. 'I still think your clients will be chasing after you!'

'Don't you believe it,' he grinned. 'No one is indispensable. That's a lesson I learned long ago.'

It was only later, when they were winging their way to India, that Julia asked Adam why he had wanted such a long honeymoon.

'Because I didn't want it to look as if our marriage was a last-minute arrangement. Rather that everything had been planned a long time ago,' he said bluntly. 'A weekend in Paris or ten days in Bermuda would have been suspect, but no one will believe I fixed this honeymoon in forty-eight hours.'

'I can't believe it myself,' she confessed. 'Miss Smith must be a genius at organising.'

'I was the genius,' he replied. 'A client of mine recommended me to a travel agent who pulled out all the stops.'

'Four weeks is a long time to be away from work,' Julia murmured. 'I hope you won't be bored.'

'I won't give myself a chance.' As if to prove his point, he picked up the book that lay on his lap, an American survey of company taxation. 'Did you bring anything to read?' he asked as an afterthought.

'Only a magazine.'

Leaning forward, he took another book from the brief-case at his feet. Expecting something that would suit his own taste, rather than hers, Julia was surprised to see it was a current best-seller.

'I had an idea you wouldn't bring anything with you,' he explained, handing it to her.

'You're very thoughtful.'

'I intend making our marriage work, Julia. I won't allow it to fail.'

'I realise that. You've always despised failure.'

'I also despise the pity that goes with it.'

She eyed him frankly, straightening in her seat to do it. 'I'm surprised you worry so much what people think of you. You're successful enough to make your own rules.'

'That's what I keep telling myself,' Adam admitted, 'but I can't make myself believe it.'

Her curiosity deepened. 'Why do you set so much store by success, Adam? Were you a failure when you were young?'

'Is this a catechism?'

'It's a question a wife might easily ask.'

'When you're my wife—in the real sense—ask me the question again.'

It was a justifiable comment, albeit a sharp one, and it surprised her, making her wonder about the past of this intelligent, autocratic man she had married. She twisted the wedding ring on her finger, unused to it, and trying not to think of it as a mark of ownership.

The flight was long and uneventful. The plane was

packed to capacity, though as Julia and Adam were
travelling first class, they had ample room. Despite this,
Julia found it tiring to sit for such a long period, and
envied Adam his ability to relax. She knew he was surprised at how little she had travelled, and she had not
bothered explaining to him that a single girl, with no
resources other than what she earned, had little opportunity of going to exotic places. For an intelligent man,
he could sometimes be very insensitive. But then, in the
moneyed circles in which he mixed, working girls with
small bank accounts did not exist.

But now I'm one of the moneyed people too, she
thought wryly, and waited to feel a thrill of pleasure. None
came, and she made herself think of the clothes she could
buy, the jewellery she could wear, the places she could
visit. But the strongest thought remained the man sitting
beside her. Adam, her husband and anxious-to-be-lover.
Hurriedly she shied away from the images this aroused in
her mind, glad no one else could see them.

It was midday when they landed in Bombay, and
nearly two hours later before they reached the Taj Mahal
Hotel, Indian Customs and Immigration being painstak-
ingly slow, and the drive from the airport exceptionally
long. But the hotel was magnificent; overlooking the
ocean and the imposing Victoria Gate, a relic of British
rule.

'I'm afraid we couldn't get into the old wing,' Adam
apologised as the lift took them up to the eighth floor of
the modern section. 'But at such short notice we were
lucky to get in at all.'

'I bet you wouldn't be happy with less than this place,'
she smiled.

'I like the best,' he agreed.

As if the words reminded him that in marrying Julia he
had accepted second best, Adam's mouth set in a hard
line which only relaxed as they entered their large suite of
rooms.

Julia, who had been worried at the prospect of sharing a bedroom with him, breathed a sigh of relief, and hearing it, he touched her arm lightly.

'You've no need to be afraid of me, Julia. I've never yet forced myself on any woman.'

Trying to hide her embarrassment, she gave him a shy glance. 'I know we agreed to wait, but this is your honeymoon and—and——'

'It's a holiday for us,' he said quickly. 'A time for us to relax and see each other as individuals, away from all outside pressures.' He looked at his watch. 'Would you like to unpack and have a rest, or do you want to freshen up and take a look at the city?'

'What would *you* like to do?'

He smiled. 'I asked the question before you did, so it has to be *your* decision. Don't forget you're my wife now, not my secretary.'

Her eyes met his. 'I think I'd like to rest.'

'Then I'll do the same. Is two hours enough?' At her nod, he walked towards his bedroom. 'I'll see you later, Julia. If there's anything you need, ring for it. The Taj pride themselves on their service.'

It was early afternoon when Julia re-entered the sitting-room that linked their two bedrooms. The decor here was lushly Mogul, with silk, down-filled cushions on well-upholstered settees, intricately patterned green and red wallpaper that matched the brocade curtains at the wide window, and a balcony that ran the full length of the suite. The air-conditioning was on and the doors were closed, and when Julia opened them and stepped outside, the heat was so intense that it physically overwhelmed her, and she quickly returned to the room.

'This is a fairly cool time of year,' Adam commented, smiling at her expression. 'It will be hotter than this in a few weeks. That's why we're starting our holiday here, instead of concluding it.'

'Where do we go from Bombay?'

'The itinerary's on the table.' He nodded towards it. 'We go to Calcutta, then up to the Plains and Kashmir, stopping at several places en route.'

'Kashmir!' Julia exclaimed. 'Oh, I've always wanted to go there. It's supposed to be breathtakingly beautiful, isn't it? Are we staying on a houseboat?'

'Yes, for a week. Then after some more sightseeing, we go on to Delhi and then home.'

'What made you choose to come to India? You don't have clients here,' she added pointedly.

'That's why I chose it,' he grinned.

Julia smiled back, aware of how boyish Adam looked when he relaxed. Normally she tended to think of him as older than his thirty-five years, and knew that he did not consider himself young. Had he done, he would never have been disturbed by the prospect of waiting four years to marry Erica and start a family. Wishing she could be as casual about love as most of her contemporaries, Julia went over to the table, picked up the itinerary and read it.

'I'm glad we'll be having a week's rest in Kashmir,' she murmured. 'We'll need it after the sightseeing on this schedule.'

'We can always cut out some of it if you get tired,' he said quickly. 'But for now, let's go down and have something to eat and then take a look at Bombay. It's supposed to be a wonderful place for shopping.'

'I'm sure you won't want to spend your holiday doing *that*!'

'Not all the time,' he agreed. 'But I know how women love buying things, and Bombay has excellent leather goods and jewellery, though Delhi is the place for material. You must buy some things for yourself, Julia. I've a fancy to see you in an exotic coloured sari.'

Recollecting that Roy had only liked her in pastels, Julia marvelled again at how different the two men were. But would Adam's sensuality be as controlled as Roy's?

'What's the matter?' Adam asked, quick to sense her agitation.

'Nothing,' she lied. 'Just a pang of hunger.'

In the weeks that followed, Julia was to see an entirely new side to the man she had married, and came to the conclusion that, like an iceberg, he kept the larger part of himself hidden, both from friends and from colleagues. Anticipating that his energy and volatile nature would make him restless on holiday, she found instead that the joie de vivre which he put into his work applied to his leisure time too. He had come away to enjoy himself and enjoy himself he was determined to do. He was an avid sightseer and, having gleaned what he could from books, encouraged their personal guides to expound at length on everything they saw and did. Finding an enthusiastic listener, the guides invariably regaled them with the past history of the country, bringing to breathtaking life every palace and monument they visited.

Julia tried and failed to see Erica enjoying this kind of holiday, and then decided that Adam would never have brought her here. Had he married the cool blonde, they would have honeymooned in a private yacht or a luxurious resort like Acapulco or Palm Beach. Yet looking at Adam as he wandered beside her, casual in shorts and open-necked shirt, his eyes alert with interest, Julia found it difficult to imagine him lying inertly on a beach for days on end.

By the time they reached Kashmir, she was exhausted by the heat and constant travel, but Adam was still full of boundless energy. His skin had tanned even darker under the hot tropical sun, and but for the fact that he was tall and broad-shouldered, he might well have been mistaken for an Indian. Julia too was tanned, and there were glints of gold in her thick auburn hair.

They had taken a plane to Srinagar, a quaint city on the banks of the River Jhelum in the Western Himalayas. Lakes abounded in the forest-covered mountains above the town, including Lake Dal where their houseboat was moored. Expecting a cabin cruiser, Julia was astonished by the size of the boat. It was a hundred and twenty feet long and twenty feet wide, and had two smaller boats attached to it: a kitchen boat for the servants, and a *shikara* boat which Adam and Julia could use if they wanted to go on expeditions to Srinagar and other nearby towns.

'I think I could live here for ever,' she said ecstatically, running from one room to another.

There were five rooms in all: three bedrooms, each with its own bathroom, and two sitting-rooms. The furniture was predominantly bamboo and covered with soft, colourful cushions. There were gay Indian rugs on the floor and billowing Indian cotton curtains at the port-holes. There was also a large terrace for sunbathing, and it was here that they sat and had a pre-dinner drink, while from the kitchen boat the delicious scent of curry and fruit wafted across to them in the breeze.

Julia was wearing a long housedress she had bought in Bombay. It was in vivid blues and greens, a dramatic foil for her glorious hair, which tonight cascaded about her shoulders.

'You should always wear your hair that way,' Adam commented, and Julia realised he had been studying her for several moments. She tried not to appear embarrassed and was glad her voice was composed when she spoke.

'I prefer my hair away from my face when it's hot.'

'Then wear it loose in the evenings,' he persisted.

'Don't you think it more sophisticated worn up?'

'I think a woman—anyone for that matter—should wear what suits her. I agree that if one ignores the fashion dictates completely, one can look strange, but so you can if you follow fashion slavishly!' He gave a wry smile. 'How portentous I sound, when all I really mean is that I like women to look feminine, and you look especially so, with your hair loose. It's a glorious colour and texture,' he added. 'Like wine-red silk.' He caught a tress between his fingers and stroked it. Then he moved his arm slightly and put his hand beneath her chin, tilting it to look into her eyes. 'Do you like it here, Julia?'

'Do you need to ask? This place is heaven.'

'And you look like one of the fallen angels in that dress,' he teased. 'It's far too sexy for heaven.'

'Sexy? But it hangs loose like a shroud.'

'Why do women always think tight-fitting clothing more provocative? Loose things leave far more to the imagination, and I'm afraid mine is running riot at the moment.'

Adam was unsmiling as he spoke, and Julia coloured hotly.

'You're even more beautiful when you blush,' he said softly, and lowering his head, placed his mouth upon hers.

She tensed, but he took no notice and gently went on caressing her lips. His tenderness was unnerving and caused a response within her she had not expected. All at once she felt vulnerable—in Adam's power—and this was something she did not want; nor did she want to show any affection towards him, aware that if it suited him, he might use it against her at some later stage.

'Why are you so nervous of me?' he whispered against her mouth.

'You took me by surprise.'

'I haven't taken you yet.'

She quivered at the implication. 'You're being too literal.'

'It's my training.'

'I hope you're well trained?'

'As a lover?' he asked.

'No, as a lawyer.'

He knew instantly what she meant, for he raised his mouth from hers and moved back. 'I don't need reminding of my promise, Julia. But you're very lovely and I found you too tempting to resist.'

Although she knew she should be flattered, she was angry that, strong-minded as he was, he could be sufficiently sexually aroused by her beauty to forget the promise he had made to her. What a prey men were to their sensual appetites! It weakened their resolve and frequently made nonsense of their intelligence.

'You're angry with me, aren't you?' he stated.

'Not with you.'

'Then with whom?'

'Men in general. They're all the same.'

She walked over to the side of the boat and stared down into the dark green waters of the lake. The Indian dusk was slowly settling around them, and fingers of purple and pink light streaked the azure sky.

'Is it only because of your ex-fiancé that you're so cynical?' Adam enquired behind her. 'One swallow doesn't make a summer, you know.'

'I'm aware of that, and it isn't only because of Roy.' Julia found it difficult to go on. She had never spoken to anyone about her parents' marriage, and was too used to hiding her feelings to express them now.

'Then what's made you such an expert on the weakness of men?' Adam persisted. 'Tell me the truth, Julia. I'm not prying from idle curiosity.'

'Aren't you?'

'Don't you know me better than that?' He moved a step, which brought him to stand at her side. 'I want our marriage to succeed, my dear, and getting to understand your fears and prejudices will help me to understand the inner you. You're still very much an enigma to me.'

'Perhaps that's part of my fascination,' she said lightly.

'And part of my frustration,' he quipped. 'A little of the unknown can be intriguing, I agree, but too much can prevent any relationship from forming.'

Julia knew he was right, and realised that if she wanted this loveless marriage to succeed, she would have to do as he said. Secrecy built barriers, and too many barriers would make it impossible for them to find contentment with each other. She bit back a sigh. What an indictment on her life that, at twenty-three, she should be willing to settle for contentment in marriage and close her mind to passion, to the heart-stopping blaze of sexual love.

'My father was a devotee of beautiful women,' she said, without turning to look at Adam. 'That's why he married my mother. She was exceptionally lovely: hair like mine, but with creamy coloured skin and absolutely classical features. She could easily have been a model for a pre-Raphaelite painting. But one beautiful woman never satisfied my father for long. He was always chasing after others, and he left her ten, twelve—oh, I don't know how many times.'

'And now you equate all men with your father?'

'Most of them, given the chance, can rarely be faithful. Roy was the same and so are you. You're in love with Erica Dukes, yet it doesn't stop you wanting to make love to *me*.'

'You're my wife, Julia,' Adam replied. 'I've no need to feel any disloyalty to Erica. I've shut her out of my mind.'

'How can you forget the woman you love?' Julia demanded, swinging round.

'I haven't forgotten her. But I refuse to live in the past. My future is with you.'

Even in the dusk Julia saw the shine in his eyes, but could not tell if it came from anger or sadness.

'I've no intention of spoiling the rest of my life because I was foolish enough to fall in love with a woman who doesn't know the meaning of the word,' he went on. 'I suppose you think I should have waited to fall in love again, but as I've already told you, I don't want that kind of emotion—any more than you do. We neither of us want to be hurt again, which is why I asked you to marry me. I've known and respected you for nearly four years, and if that doesn't lead to a good marriage, then nothing will.'

'How rational you make everything sound! Yet when you kissed me just now, I felt cheap.'

Adam's breath drew in sharply. 'I'm sorry you find my kisses demeaning,' he said. 'Most women would have been flattered.' He put up his hand to stop her replying. 'And please don't say you're not like most women. I know that already—otherwise I wouldn't have married you.'

In a way it was an apology, and Julia accepted it, knowing he did not often admit he was in the wrong, even to his closest friends.

'Don't be angry with me, Adam,' she said huskily. 'But everything seems so unreal—our marriage and my being here with you. It will take me time to get used to it. After all, you've been my employer for so long, it isn't easy to start thinking of you as my husband. It still seems like a dream.'

'Then don't turn it into a nightmare, or me into an ogre. I'm a very ordinary, normal man.'

'Normal, I agree,' she smiled, 'but I would never call you ordinary.'

'At which point I suggest we go in for dinner,' Adam said, smiling, giving her his arm.

Together they walked across the deck to the dining room. Through the open doorway Julia saw the beautifully laid table. Candles had been lit, casting their soft radiance on polished wood, exotic flowers and the mellow glow of brass cutlery.

'You could almost call this place our first home,' Adam murmured. 'But as we're still keeping our marriage platonic, I won't suggest carrying you over the threshold!'

CHAPTER FIVE

JULIA's return to London, after her honeymoon with Adam, marked the start of a completely new life. She still found it hard to envisage a permanent future with him and, as she wandered through his beautiful Chester Street house, again marvelled that she had got herself into this situation. Would she ever be able to regard this place as her home? How would she cope with the domestic staff and fit into her role as Adam's hostess? They were questions which worried her deeply, yet she dared not burden him with them. He believed her to be capable and confident, and she had no intention of letting him know how disturbed she was. Besides, he wouldn't care; his only concern was that she put on a convincing performance.

Since the night on the houseboat in Kashmir, Adam had not overstepped the boundaries of propriety. In fact he had been so restrained that it had been almost like holidaying with a brother. His camaraderie had helped to loosen her nervousness with him, and though she was still conscious of the social and educational differences between them, she knew these were fast beginning to matter less and less. Which was as it should be. In her own right, Julia knew she could contribute as much to their marriage as Adam: her calm, her sympathy, her understanding of the moods that swayed him during his hectic hours of work, were what turned a girl-friend into a beloved wife. Except that she had never been the girl-friend and was unlikely ever to be anything more than his beloved substitute.

Once back at work, Adam had quickly reverted to his role as the dynamic, supercharged international lawyer. Until their marriage Julia had only seen his behaviour in the office, but living with him, she soon realised that even when away from it, he was always mulling over the day's events.

'Don't you ever get tired of wheeling and dealing?' she asked him at the end of their first week at home.

'Wheeling and dealing?' he queried. 'You make me sound a rather dubious character!'

'Well, you're the only lawyer I know who advises his clients on how to run their businesses, and then goes and works with their rivals!'

'Only so that I can introduce "the rivals" to my clients,' Adam reminded her with a smile. 'Companies spend far too much time in competition with one another, instead of joining forces to maximise their strength.'

'Are you advocating monopolies?'

'To a limited extent.' His smile widened into a grin. 'In Britain, we call it nationalisation.'

Julia sniffed. 'I can see you entering politics one day.'

'Business politics only. Never the government kind. They're too dirty for me.'

As she walked into his study and saw his desk neatly piled with legal documents, Julia remembered this conversation. There was a ruthless side to Adam which she was sure made him the perfect negotiator, and his sharp brain made her feel inadequate. How would it be five years from now, she wondered, when they had had the family he hoped for? Would their children's emotional development be affected by the loveless marriage of their parents? Adam had said he believed it would not matter for children to have parents who were not in love, provided they respected one another, and recalling her mother and father, Julia conceded that this might be true.

Yet intimacy with Adam was something she was not ready to think about. They had been married a month, and he would soon expect her to be his wife in the fullest sense of the word. It was a discomfiting thought, and it haunted her as she sat opposite him at dinner that night.

Glancing around the beautifully furnished Chippendale room, she knew what a splendid picture they made of gracious living. How handsome Adam looked in a black silk sweater and suede pants. It was the sort of casual yet elegant attire she had grown used to his wearing. His clothes always looked so right on him.

'It's pleasant coming back to English food,' he commented, sipping at his iced Vichyssoise.

'You mean French food,' she laughed. 'What would Monsieur Romain say if he heard you call it English?'

'Which reminds me,' said Adam, putting down his spoon. 'Romain has been with me for five years—he's the best chef I've ever had, so I'd like him and his wife to stay. But you can make your own decisions regarding the rest of the staff, and you can fire and hire at will.'

'I wouldn't dream of doing any such thing,' Julia protested. 'From what I've seen, your home is perfectly run.'

'*Our* home, Julia. Not only mine.' Adam continued drinking his soup. 'By the way, I've opened an account for you at the bank. You'll be getting a quarterly allowance.'

Uncomfortably, she avoided his gaze. 'You needn't have done that. I've some money of my own.'

'A private income?' he asked, surprised.

'No. Only the money I've saved since I've been working. But it amounts to quite a bit.'

Adam shrugged, and Julia's temper rose. 'I know it wouldn't seem much to you, but——'

'Let's not argue about money, Julia,' he interposed. 'I'm sure we'll find a great many other things to quarrel about, but it need never be over something as unimportant as money.'

'I'm amazed that you regard it as unimportant,' she said tartly, 'when it cost you your marriage to Mrs Dukes.'

Only as she heard her words aloud did Julia regret her

cheap jibe. She had no right to hurt Adam because of Erica Dukes' behaviour, nor to be angry because he wanted to give his wife an allowance. As a feminist, she should see it as legal payment for her contribution to their marriage, and not as something that made her dependent on him.

'I'm sorry,' she said contritely. 'What I just said was cruel and stupid.'

'Not stupid, Julia. But unnecessarily cruel. If you're going to be on the defensive with me the whole time, it will make things doubly hard for both of us.'

'I realise that,' she replied, 'and I promise it won't happen again.'

'I'm sure it will.' There was irony in Adam's voice. 'You have too much red in that glorious hair of yours for you always to control your tongue.'

She swallowed the reply that rose to her lips, then glancing at the dress she was wearing, said: 'Do you want me to buy a different kind of clothes? French or Italian, perhaps?'

'Buy what you like. You have excellent taste, though I think you should let yourself go a little, colourwise.'

She made a face at him. 'You like me in bright colours, don't you?'

'I like you in pastels too. But I think you should play up to your hair and eyes and be more dramatic.'

Remembering the cool blonde looks of the woman he loved, Julia surmised that Adam wished his wife to be the exact opposite, and vowed to knock him in the eye with the next outfit she bought.

'Don't buy any furs or jewellery,' he cut into her thoughts. 'That's my prerogative.'

'I wasn't thinking of it,' she said humorously. 'I've never had a fur in my life.'

'Would you prefer mink or sable?'

'Neither. I don't fancy having animals skinned for my edification.'

'You aren't a vegetarian, though.'

How quick Adam was with the rapier reply, she thought, and gave a wry grimace. 'You're right, of course, but if I actually start thinking of baby lambs being killed to provide me with tender chops, I'd throw up.'

'So you don't think about it, and you go on eating meat,' he replied, refilling their wine glasses. 'Which is what I suggest you do when it comes to furs.'

'No!' Her retort was sharp, and startled him. But Julia had had enough of his reasoned arguments. 'I know I'm not being logical, Adam, but that can't be helped. I'll go on eating meat, but I positively refuse to wear furs.'

'You've no objection to jewellery, though?' He pursed his lips as she shook her head. 'Thank God for that! So we'll settle for diamonds and sapphires.'

'Must we?'

'Just a few pieces. My friends will expect it.'

'Do you run the whole of your life to suit your friends?' she questioned, and was pleased to see him look disconcerted.

'Stop hitting me below the belt, Julia. None of us can live in limbo, and we're all affected by what other people think and do. After all, your own attitude to yourself and the distrust you have of men stems from your inability to ignore *one* man's behaviour.'

Her face flamed. 'Now *you're* hitting below the belt!'

'It's a game that two can play, my dear. Remember that.'

'You sound just like a husband.'

'I wish I was,' he said abruptly. 'I never thought you'd act like a frightened virgin, but I suppose in an odd sort of way, I'm glad.'

Later, thinking back over the conversation, Julia was irritated. Frightened virgin, indeed! Yet he'd then confused her by saying he was pleased she was untouched. It was an attitude that obviously did not extend to Erica, who was the exact opposite. How strange people were:

saying one thing and then showing by their actions that they meant something quite different. Julia wondered what it would be like to be touched by Adam. She felt sure he would be as adept at lovemaking as he was at everything else he did. But she wanted more than just a skilful lover; she wanted a loving husband.

'Then you shouldn't have married Adam Lester,' a little voice inside her said. 'You're not being logical, Julia Gosford, now Julia Lester.'

But how could a jilted girl be expected to think logically?

However, her memories of Roy were fading, and she was able to look more dispassionately at her life. There was no turning back the clock; this she accepted. On the other hand, would she want to, even if she could? As Adam had said, a marriage built on mutual understanding and common interest had a good chance of survival. And when they were in India, she had discovered that she and Adam did like the same things in sculpture, art, books and food.

'We'll go to Italy next,' he had said. 'Until you've seen the galleries in Florence and Venice, you've seen nothing.'

Lying in bed, Julia wished she and Adam could leave this house again and wander the hill towns of Central Italy, with their fabulous churches and art collections. In London, he was fast becoming remote again, so immersed in his work that he occasionally acted as if he resented coming home. She thought of him lying in the next room, and wondered whether he would behave differently if their marriage was a real one. Somehow she thought he might.

Sighing, she punched her pillow into another position and tried to count sheep. But still it eluded her, and again she thought of the man who lay so close to her, yet who was, emotionally, far away. Julia knew he wanted to make love to her, and wished she could understand why she was reluctant to let him. It wasn't as if she didn't find him attractive. On the contrary. There had been many times during their honeymoon when she had nearly given herself to him, and had only been prevented from doing so by the memory of Erica.

Unbidden, Roy came into her mind. Had he already married his Canadian girl-friend, or was he, as usual, being cautious; weighing up carefully all the pros and cons as befitted an actuary, bringing the clear-headedness and precision of his profession into his private life? She wouldn't be surprised to discover that the Canadian girl had a rich father who would be useful to him in his career. Thinking with more dispassion about Roy, she was fast beginning to see that Adam was a far warmer person.

When Julia went down for breakfast next morning, Adam had not yet left for the office.

'Are you always up this early?' he asked, as she came into the dining room.

'Even earlier when I worked for you.'

'But now you can take it easy.'

'Force of habit,' she shrugged. 'But I must say I wish you hadn't asked me to stop work. I'm going to die of boredom.'

'I'm sure there are lots of things you could do to occupy yourself.'

'Not charity committees,' Julia replied with a shudder. 'Maybe I'll take a job with someone else. One of your rivals, perhaps?'

'I don't recognise any!'

'How conceited you are,' she teased.

'I wouldn't call knowing your value conceit,' he answered seriously. 'People tend to take you at your own estimation, so always think well of yourself.' He regarded her housecoat, a simple tunic in sprigged cotton. 'Something silky and floating would suit you better.'

'This is more practical.'

'You don't need to be practical any longer.' His mouth

quirked. 'You aren't washing the dishes any more.'

'True enough,' she said evenly. 'Perhaps I'll go out shopping instead, and fritter away your money.'

'An excellent idea. Buy yourself some evening dresses, and something suitable for the country, too. Also some smart day dresses. You'll occasionally be lunching with me.'

'Why?'

'My foreign clients often bring their wives with them, and I'll expect you to entertain the women.'

'Is that one of the reasons you wanted a wife?'

'It never occurred to me until now,' he replied. 'But you're very good with people—I noticed it in the office—and as you've complained of having nothing to do . . .'

'Would you have asked Erica to do it too?'

Adam's tanned face suffused with colour, but he banged his coffee cup on the saucer. 'Must you constantly bring Erica into our conversation?'

'I'm sorry!' Julia was embarrassed. 'But she's often in my mind and . . .'

'I can't imagine why,' he cut across her.

Neither could Julia, but now was not the time to puzzle out the reason.

'Since you've mentioned her name,' Adam continued, 'I think we should invite her to dinner. I want to give a party, and I'll let you have a list of the other people we should ask.'

'Do we have to invite Mrs Duke?'

'Yes—if we don't want gossip. I saw her a great deal in the past, and my friends will think it strange if I were suddenly to drop her.'

'It's possible they'd think you were in love with your wife,' Julia said with unconcealed sarcasm. 'Men don't usually continue seeing their ex-girl-friends, once they've parted.'

'It depends on the parting.' His lids lowered, making

the expression in his eyes difficult to read. 'But I'd still like to ask her over.'

'She might refuse,' said Julia, recalling Erica's fury when she had last seen her in the office.

'I'm sure she won't, if only to show everyone she doesn't give a damn about me.' He paused. 'You don't really mind her coming here, do you?'

'Why should I? She means nothing to *me*. How soon do you want the dinner party?' Julia went on, as Adam pushed back his chair and rose.

'Ring Miss Smith and ask her when I'm free.' He saw Julia's look of surprise. 'I go abroad quite often, remember?'

'For a moment I thought you meant you'd be going out in the evenings.'

'And leave you alone at night?' Adam replied. 'We're newlyweds and supposed to be in love.' He paused by the door. 'Let's have the dinner party as soon as possible.'

That day, Julia made all the arrangements: contacting the people Adam wanted and discussing the menu with Romain. She was reluctant to telephone Erica, and debated whether to write, then told herself off for being chicken, and made the call.

To her relief the woman was out for the day, and Julia explained the reason for calling and left her number, hoping she would not be in either when her call was returned.

In the early afternoon she left the house to go shopping, and as she reached the end of the road, she looked back. She still found it incredible to think she lived in such opulent surroundings. How happy her mother would have been for her; not only because of Adam's position, but because a man who was so determined that his marriage should work would not indulge in affairs. Julia was warmed by the knowledge. Although she did not love Adam, it was good to know he would not get involved with anyone else. On the other hand he did not expect to remain celibate, and this put the ball firmly in her own court.

At that moment an empty taxi slowed in front of her, and she climbed in and told the driver to take her to the boutique in Mayfair which Adam had recommended, deciding that for the rest of the day she would concentrate on making herself into the image her husband wanted. When she would eventually decide to become his lover was a decision for another day.

It was late when Julia returned home, laden with dress boxes, and even later by the time she had made herself ready to meet Adam. But the look on his face as she entered the drawing room was compensation enough for the three hours of fittings and the endless deliberations as to whether she should take this dress or that. Who would have thought spending money could be as tiring as earning it!

If Julia had had any doubts about the cobalt blue dress that fitted her figure like a second skin, or been worried that her new hair-style—long and softly curled around her face—would meet with Adam's approval, his astonished silence as she saw her was assurance enough.

'You look stunning,' he said slowly. 'Simply beautiful.'

'Expensively beautiful,' she corrected lightly. 'I've spent all of my quarterly allowance.'

'I'll put some more money in your account tomorrow.' He studied her hair, then reached out and touched it with his fingers. 'It feels like silk. I've never seen such a wonderful texture.'

Gently he went on stroking it, and Julia had an unaccountable urge to take his fingers in her own. Quickly she controlled it, and said rather sharply: 'You make me feel as if I'm a doll on display.'

'Not a doll,' he said huskily. 'Very much a woman.'

'Don't you mean a possession? Something you can show off and then put back on the shelf while you attend to other things?'

'You *are* in a mood,' he remarked, stepping back from her. 'You must have had a tiring day. Sit down and I'll fix you a drink. What would you like?'

'Champagne, of course,' she said sarcastically.

He chuckled. 'You aren't going to arouse my temper, Julia. I'm in too good a mood.' He handed her a glass of champagne and then settled in a chair with a whisky. 'I'm glad you've organised the dinner party. Erica rang me at the office to say she could come.'

'I'm delighted to hear it.'

Adam's look was quizzical. It flattered his features, accentuating the sensual curve of his mouth and the sharp glint in his eyes.

'You could easily give the impression that you're jealous of her,' he said softly.

Julia laughed. 'After four years of working for you, and thinking of you as my boss, it'll take longer than six weeks for me to see you in any romantic light.'

'I've heard of stranger things happening,' he said slyly. 'People have been known to fall in love overnight.'

'You don't need anyone to love you,' she retorted. 'Only someone to go to bed with you.'

'Shall we change the subject?' he asked quietly. 'As I've just said, I'm in too relaxed a mood to trade insults with you.'

Later that night as Julia undressed for bed, she decided it would suit Adam very well were she to fall in love with him. It would make her like putty in his hands, which she was determined not to be. Although Adam had been an excellent employer and was now a pleasant companion—when she was not riling him over Erica—he was not the sort of man she could love. He would demand and expect total submission, and she had already seen what that could do to a woman. What colossal nerve he had, to think she might fall for him! If only she had had the courage to suggest it might be the other way around—that he might fall in love with *her*.

That would have given him plenty of food for thought.

Unexpectedly it gave Julia food for thought too, and she tossed restlessly in bed. Was it possible, she wondered, to close one's heart to love? Yet didn't a hot, languorous night like this make one realise the futility of fighting one's senses? Why shouldn't she concede to sex without love? Eventually she would have to do so, if she kept her word. Yet right now the very idea of it still horrified her.

Agitated, she sat up, her body trembling. She couldn't go on with this farcical marriage. She didn't want Adam to hold her and kiss her while his mind and body yearned for another woman. Hard on this thought came another; one that set her trembling even more. Would she want Adam if he no longer desired another woman? If he only wanted herself? No, she thought in a panic. No, I wouldn't. He's too overpowering, too confident. Yet not so confident that he could take Erica's rebuff without feeling the need to prove she hadn't hurt him by instantly marrying someone else.

'I'm a symbol of his weakness,' Julia whispered to herself. 'Every time he looks at me, I'm sure he remembers that. And as long as he does, he'll never be able to see me as I really am.'

CHAPTER SIX

IF Adam managed to fool his friends by marrying Julia, he certainly did not fool himself. Although Julia was an extremely beautiful and desirable girl, it was the memory of Erica's Nordic fairness that still tortured him. He tried, with all his logic, to analyse her attraction, thinking of her faults as well as her virtues. It seemed to work, for he found that after a while he could regard her with more dispassion—and therefore be more critical—and when she rang him at his office to accept their dinner invitation, he was able to speak to her without feeling any kind of emotion. It was truly a triumph of mind over matter, and he was particularly pleased with himself.

He remembered the way he had accused Julia of being jealous of Erica, and knew he had done her an injustice, for his wife in name only had never experienced deep passions for anyone, of that he was sure. She had told him she loved Roy, but Adam was prepared to swear it was a very milk-and-water kind of emotion; definitely not the all-consuming love that gave no peace to the mind.

How would Julia behave if she really went overboard for a man? he wondered. Some day it might happen, and when it did he was determined to make certain she was looking in his direction. At this precise moment she was an admirable companion, ready to use her considerable organising talents to ensure that his home and social life ran smoothly. But if she loved him she would make a wonderful wife: passionate, pliable, loving; exactly what he wanted. He knew he was thinking as a chauvinist, but it had the redeeming feature of being an honest admission.

Within a day of their first dinner party being arranged,

Adam flew to Cairo on business, and did not return home until the day of the party. Entering the house, he was immediately aware of something different. Julia had bought a mass of plants, and a leafy palm in a mellow bronze tub brightened the dark well of the staircase. Bowls of fresh flowers stood on the occasional tables in the drawing room, and all their furniture had been rearranged. The two settees now faced each other on either side of the fireplace, instead of being at opposite ends of the room, and the chairs had been placed in several groups, to make more intimate conversation pieces.

Adam stood in the middle of the room and surveyed it with approval. Yes, Julia was settling down well, and he was proud of himself for having made such a good choice in marrying her. There was a warmth and lived-in quality pervading the house which had not previously been present. Erica's home, though beautiful, had looked like a decorator's showcase. Adam frowned, annoyed that such a thought should cross his mind. It was foolhardy to compare the two women. Not only were they dissimilar in looks, but also in character, and one did not fall in love with someone because of character. Rather it was an inexplicable pull of the senses.

Abruptly he strode into the hall and up the stairs. He was passing Julia's door when it opened and she stepped out, nearly bumping into him.

'Watch out!' he smiled, putting up a steadying hand.

'My fault,' she said. 'When did you get back? Miss Smith didn't know what time you were due in at the office.'

'I'd no intention of going back there. I came here straight from the airport.'

'It's not like you to play truant.'

'Truant?' His eyebrows rose. 'Try flying to Cairo and back in three days, with business meetings as your only relaxation! I couldn't wait to get home.'

'I just wondered,' Julia said mildly. 'In the past, you've

always returned to the office first.'

'Things are different now, my dear. After all, I have a
wife waiting for me. Incidentally, you've done wonders
with the drawing room and the hall.'

'Thank you,' she said coolly. 'But there's no need to go
overboard with your praise. Nor do you need play the
part of the considerate husband when we're alone
together.'

Adam hid his irritation. He had especially come direct
from the airport to give Julia moral support before her
first dinner party, but from her composed manner it
seemed he had misjudged what her mood would be.

'I'll see to the wines,' he said abruptly.

'I've already done it.'

'The choice of wine is usually the man's prerogative.'

'I didn't know what time you'd be back, so I had the
claret brought up from the cellar this morning. Otherwise
it would have been too cold. If you had wanted to choose
the wines yourself, you should have done something about
it before going away.'

'I had other things on my mind.'

'I realise that; which is why I did it for you.' Julia's
glance was steady. 'All I'm trying to do is show you I can
manage your home perfectly well.'

With a mutter, Adam retired to his bedroom. He made
no attempt to work out why he was irritated, deciding it
was due to the journey and fatigue. This seemed to be
borne out by the fact that a warm bath and a nap soon
soothed his ruffled spirits, especially when, on waking, he
found a thermos of coffee and a plate of smoked salmon
sandwiches on his bedside table. Julia really was a jewel.
In some ways it was a pity she had married him. She
deserved someone who could love her, not a man who
had vowed never to love again. This reminder of Erica
disturbed him, and he stared for several moments into
space, willing himself to relax. Then he poured himself

another cup of coffee, drank it at a gulp and dropped off
to sleep again.

The sound of Julia's door closing re-awakened him with
a start. It was six-thirty and he guessed she had come up
to bathe and change. He decided to go in and talk to her,
and was halfway out of bed when he reminded himself
that he had no right to intrude on her privacy. He
grimaced at the door. It was an amazing situation. To
think that in this day and age he should be living platoni-
cally with his beautiful bride! And there was no denying
Julia was beautiful. It was something he had only become
aware of the night he had taken her to the opera. Before
that she had been an impersonal shadow. I was like a
horse with blinkers, he mused, seeing only what I wanted
to see. Yet it was these very blinkers that had made him
the singleminded and remarkably successful man he was.

It was a pity his grandfather couldn't see him now. He
wouldn't look down his beaky nose at him today, as he
had done when Adam was a child.

'Stop looking so scared, and for God's sake stop snivel-
ling!' the old man had often barked. 'Heaven knows
what's going to become of you. You'll probably bring dis-
grace to the family, like your mother did, or end up a
penniless rogue like your father.'

How insensitive and bigoted his grandfather had been,
puffed up with false pride and prejudice. Adam had
vowed early on that the old man would live to regret his
words. Unfortunately his grandfather had died before
Adam could prove how wrong his dire predictions had
been. Yet it was the old man's taunting that had been the
catalyst. For many, fame was the spur, but for Adam it
had been his grandfather's belief that his tenth and most
unloved grandchild would be a hopeless failure.

There was a knock on the door.

'Come in,' he called, and Julia did.

It was a Julia he had never seen before: a radiant creature in pale pink chiffon. The floating lines of the skirt

gave her added height, and the softly draped neckline
showed her creamy shoulders to perfection. To suit the
Winterhalter look of her dress, she had brushed her hair
from her face, and long curls fell down one side of her
neck. Her azure blue eyes, fringed with their incredibly
long lashes, lowered modestly and then lifted again.

'Well, Adam, do you like my dress?'

Her voice sounded shaky and he sensed she was not as
composed as he had thought. It was not surprising. Any
bride would find it an ordeal to give her first dinner party
for her husband's friends. And how much more so for
Julia, in the strange situation she was in.

'You look beautiful,' he said gently.

'Honestly?'

'Cub's honour.'

'Why not a scout?'

'If I allowed myself to believe I was old enough to be a
scout,' he said gravely, 'I'd lock the door and make a
lunge for you!'

She chuckled, and her tension eased.

'That's better,' Adam smiled. 'Give me ten minutes to
dress and then we can have a quiet drink together before
our guests arrive.'

She turned to leave, and the smooth curves of her
shoulders and the paler skin at the nape of her neck looked
so vulnerable that Adam longed to reach out and comfort
her. He was surprised by his reaction, for he rarely felt
tenderness towards anyone. Yet Julia, for all her reserve
and pride, was a gentle girl who had not deserved to be
hurt by the pompous ass with whom she had fallen in
love. She needed a man to protect her; to show her that
the opposite sex were not all flawed like her father.

'Julia,' he said abruptly, and she turned and glanced
round at him, her face so expressionless that he lost the
impulse to confide his thoughts. 'It's nothing,' he finished.
'Just a passing thought that isn't worth mentioning.'

By eight-thirty all the guests except Erica had arrived,

and Adam signalled for another round of drinks to be served. Erica detested unpunctuality and he was sure she had deliberately chosen to be late, using this method to show she didn't give a damn how many eyes watched her make her entrance and greet the wife of the man who, until a short time ago, had been her lover. It was a courageous thing for her to do, and he could not help but admire it.

At nine o'clock, Julia drifted casually over to him, the smile on her lips not echoed in her eyes.

'All our guests are here except Erica,' she said in a low voice. 'If I delay dinner any longer, it will be ruined.'

'Give Erica another five minutes,' he said. 'If she isn't here by——' Adam broke off as he glimpsed Erica's silvery blonde head in the hall, and with a murmur of apology, he went out to greet her.

'I hope I'm not too late?' she said coolly, slipping off her mink jacket and handing it to the butler.

'You know you are, and you don't care,' said Adam with a sharp smile. 'But better late than never.'

'I'd have thought you'd have wanted it to be "never",' Erica replied. 'I didn't expect to be invited here again. Where's your secretary?'

Adam stiffened. 'I've no idea. But I'd like you to meet my wife.'

'How loyal you are,' Erica mocked.

'I'd have been loyal to you, if you'd married me.'

'But not loyal enough to wait four years.'

'You know why I married Julia.'

'To have children while you were still young enough to enjoy them? Don't give me that story, Adam. You were furious that I put money before marriage, and you were too proud to remain in my life as my lover.'

Ignoring the comment, Adam motioned Erica to precede him into the room, then guided her towards Julia, who was talking to Jack Burglass. The two women were a perfect foil for one another—Julia, voluptuous and sultry;

Erica, fragile as a sliver of glass. Adam tried to look at them without prejudice, and wondered which one he would choose were he to meet them both today, for the first time. It was a fanciful question, for he already had the answer. Erica, naturally. Yet to be honest, Julia had a great deal going for her too. Once again he studied both women.

Fire and ice. It was an apt description, and each had its merits. Coolness to help one relax; to bring calm and tranquillity before the sudden shock of raw passion. His eyes were caught by a dark red ringlet. Fire to bring warmth that would help a tired man unwind; warmth that would lead to succour and satisfaction. Julia half-turned and he saw the curve of her breasts. Satisfaction and love; for only with love would Julia surrender. He bit back a sigh. The man in her life would have much to be thankful for.

'It was sweet of you to invite me here, Julia,' Erica was saying. 'I know Adam so well, I feel as if I'm already a friend of yours.'

'We met quite a few times at the office,' Julia replied with composure.

'Did we?' The dark eyes were innocent. 'I must confess I never noticed you.'

'That's the sign of a good secretary,' Julia replied equably. 'Service with anonymity.'

'What say we go in to dinner?' Adam put in, edgy at where the conversation might lead.

'Of course, darling,' Julia agreed, and gave a sign to the butler, who opened the double doors leading into the dining room.

As they took their places at the table, Adam was surprised to see that Julia had placed Erica on his right.

'How diplomatic of your secretary to have me as guest of honour,' Erica murmured to him.

'My wife has many virtues.'

'You don't expect me to believe she's *really* your wife, do you?'

Knowing it was impossible to continue this conversation quietly, Adam turned his attention to the woman on his left. He supposed he should be pleased that Erica was upset by his marriage, yet all he felt was a great sadness that they should both have wasted their lives. From the corner of his eye he saw the sparkle of diamonds around her throat, and the magnificent rings on her fingers, and it reminded him that she regarded money as more important than love. He raised his wine glass and, looking down the table, saw that Julia had raised hers. He tried to catch her glance so that he could toast her with his eyes, but she was too absorbed in conversation to look his way. Perhaps it was better that she hadn't, he mused, for she might have seen his desire to toast her as an act put on for Erica's benefit.

'I want to talk to you privately, Adam,' Erica whispered.

'What's the point?' he asked.

'At one time you'd never ask a question like that!'

'I never used to be married.'

Erica's delicate mouth tightened into a thin line, and he said quickly: 'Very well. I'll see you in my study, after dinner.'

Instantly Erica relaxed, her mouth becoming soft again. It looked prettier that way, and Adam was surprised she should allow her inner feelings to show through and spoil her beauty. Yet Julia's mouth didn't look ugly when she was annoyed. If anything, it looked more kissable. Dismayed by such disloyal thoughts, he concentrated on the conversation around him. He wanted his marriage to be a real one, but he definitely didn't want it to be confused by love. From now on, no woman would possess him emotionally, which meant he had to ensure that he didn't turn to Julia on the rebound.

Dinner over, Julia led the women into the drawing room, and Erica raised her eyebrows at him as she followed them. Adam gave no sign of seeing it, and remained at the table while the port was passed, then excused himself by saying he had an urgent telephone call to make.

As he walked down the corridor to his study, he felt so ill at ease that he knew subterfuge was not his scene. In his professional life he could resort to it without qualm, but not in his personal life. Not only did he want things to look right, he wanted them to be right. And that meant making his marriage a real one. The sooner he and Julia lived together as man and wife, the easier their relationship would be, and the tormenting love he had once had for Erica would become a thing of the past.

Had once had? Adam faltered a step. Why was he using the past tense? Was it an accident of thought or had his subconscious come to the fore? Opening the study door, he went in. Erica was already there, standing in front of the hearth and looking like a pale lily in her cream chiffon dress. Of course he still loved her. The fact that his pulse did not leap at sight of her only meant his feelings were under control.

'Adam!' She glided over and rested her face against his chest.

Automatically his arms came around her and he felt the delicate bones of her body.

'I love you,' she whispered, 'and I hate you for not waiting.'

'I told you I wasn't prepared to lose four years of my life.'

'You've still lost them,' she retorted. 'When the four years are up, you'll come back to me.'

'No, I won't. I have a wife now, and I soon hope to have children.'

'Children?' Erica pulled sharply away from him. 'Don't expect me to believe your marriage is real!'

'Facts will speak for themselves.'

Once again the delicate mouth became thin and ugly. 'You mean you're prepared to go to bed with a girl you don't love, in order to prove to your friends how happy you are?' she said sarcastically.

'I *am* happy,' he replied. 'Did you expect me to mourn you for ever?'

'Yes, I did,' Erica cried. 'You'll never forget me, no matter how hard you try. I'm your kind of woman, Adam.'

'Not any more. At one time I thought you were, but I soon discovered I was wrong.'

'And you'll find you're wrong again.'

'No,' he denied. 'You turned me down once, and you won't get another chance.'

'Won't I?' she said huskily, and stepped close to him again.

As she pressed her body against his, memories of the passionate hours they had spent together made Adam a traitor to the present, and he could not stop the surge of desire that swept over him.

'You see!' Erica cried, moving her hands lightly down his chest, to pause by the throbbing muscles that ridged his thighs. 'You *do* want me, Adam. You do!'

'You're an easy woman to want,' he said heavily. 'But wanting isn't loving.'

'Don't tell me you love your secretary?'

'I love her honesty and sincerity. That's a better basis for marriage than *we* would have had.' Pushing Erica away from him, Adam moved to the door. 'If you'll excuse me, I should get back to my guests.'

'You're running away because you're afraid of me,' Erica whispered, gliding towards him. 'But you needn't be, Adam. You're the only man I'll ever love, and I intend having you *and* Kenneth's money.'

'Never,' he said harshly. But Erica didn't hear him because she had already gone from the room.

With a sigh Adam made his way down the corridor. How convinced Erica was of her ability to get him back! Yet he was equally sure she wouldn't, for somehow his love for her had diminished. Was it because he had deliberately frozen his emotions to avoid further pain, or was it a genuine lessening of desire? He wished he knew the answer, but now was not the time to puzzle it out. Forcing a smile to his lips, he went back into the dining room.

It was nearly one o'clock when the party broke up, and with the departure of the last guest, Julia visibly wilted. It was like watching a light go out, and again Adam was overwhelmed by an inexplicable surge of tenderness towards her, and a longing to lift her up in his arms and carry her to her room. How he wished it were 'their' room! He rubbed the side of his face. He had promised to wait until she was ready for him, but he doubted if this would ever happen; each step forward was followed by two steps back, with Erica the force that was pushing them apart.

'Come into the study and relax for a while,' he suggested. 'It'll do you good to sit quietly before going to bed.'

Julia hesitated, but then slowly followed him.

'You don't often come in here, do you, Julia?' he asked, as they entered the study.

'I don't feel I have the right. This is very much your room, Adam. You wouldn't want it filled with memories of me.'

'Memories?' he echoed. 'You speak as if you're going away.'

'You wouldn't miss me if I did.'

'We made a bargain,' he pointed out, and immediately knew from her expression that he had said the wrong thing. 'I wasn't trying to remind you of it, Julia. It was just my clumsy way of saying I'd miss you.'

She shrugged in disbelief, and he decided to let the subject drop. Crossing to his desk, he returned with a bar of chocolate, which he handed to her. She looked at him with such surprise that he chuckled.

'I thought you might be hungry. I noticed you hardly

touched your dinner, and it's my bet you're depressed because of a lack of sugar.'

Julia was amused. 'Trust you to find a practical reason for my blues!' She broke the chocolate bar and offered him half.

'I don't need it,' he said.

'Yes, you do. You're too thin.'

'I'm strong as a horse.' Adam playfully flexed his muscles and Julia stepped quickly away from him, disguising the sudden movement by settling at once into a chair. Her skirt billowed around her and she looked as if she were sitting on a pale pink cloud.

'You should be feeling very pleased with yourself, Julia.' Adam was surprised that his voice sounded husky, and he cleared his throat. 'The dinner was perfect, and so were you.'

'Perfect is one of your favourite words.'

'You make it sound like an indictment!'

'Maybe it is,' she replied. 'Most people find it impossible to be perfect. Perhaps one day you'll learn to make allowances for them.'

'I've already done so—many times. Otherwise I'd have no friends.'

'Yet *you* want to be perfect.'

'I think you're using the wrong word.' He came closer to her. 'Success is probably a better one. It's failure I abhor. Any kind of failure.' He looked at Julia questioningly. 'Does that make me less admirable in your eyes?'

'Yes,' she said promptly. 'Not everyone can be a success, Adam, and even failure has its compensations. Some of the nicest people I know are failures.'

'You're being charitable.'

'I think not.'

'Except to me,' he added softly, and with a sudden movement, pulled her up into his arms. Instantly she tried to draw back, but he refused to let her go. 'Doesn't a husband have the right to say thank you to his wife for a perfect dinner party?' he whispered, and not giving her a chance to reply, pressed his mouth upon hers.

Her lips remained unyielding, and when he tried to force them apart she beat her hands angrily upon his chest. Ignoring her temper, he went on kissing her, moving his own hands slowly across her back and down the firm line of her spine; over the smooth curves of her hips and up to the fuller swell of her breasts. She began to tremble, and he knew instinctively that she was not unmoved by what he was doing, even though she was desperately fighting against it.

'Kiss me,' he whispered, pushing aside the folds of chiffon covering her breasts, to touch the nipples that were standing firmly erect. God! she wanted him as much as he wanted her. Why didn't she realise it and relax with him? 'Kiss me,' he repeated.

'No!'

'Why not?' He rubbed his cheek against hers. 'Open your mouth and kiss me, Julia. It's time you stopped being shy with me. We've already been married two months.'

With a suddenness that took him unawares, she pulled away from him. 'Must you always keep referring to our bargain?' she asked indignantly. 'You told me you'd wait till I was ready, and I'm not. I don't feel I can—I can——'

'Sacrifice yourself?' he cut in bitterly.

'Yes,' she said. 'That's what it will be—a sacrifice. Do you think I want to be touched by a man who's constantly thinking of another woman?'

'Leave Erica out of this,' Adam said angrily.

'How can I? You make it impossible. Do you think I didn't notice her disappearing from the drawing room after dinner, and then coming back looking like the cat that had swallowed the canary?'

'I can assure you *I* wasn't the canary.'

'But you won't deny you were with her?'

'Of course I was with her. But only because I was

worried she'd make a scene if I said no.'

'Do you still love her?'

Before tonight, Adam would unhesitatingly have said 'yes'. But seeing Erica after a lapse of nearly two months, he was no longer sure. She still aroused him, yet he had been much more critical of her behaviour; had actually found himself noticing and disliking her antagonism.

'Don't bother answering my question,' Julia said into the silence, and before he could explain why he had taken so long, she pushed past him and ran from the room.

Adam sat down in the chair she had vacated. The perfume she wore still hovered around it, and he breathed it in. Without rhyme or reason he felt unbearably saddened, and knew a deep longing to hold her in his arms again and caress her beautiful skin. Habit was a powerful force. In the last eight weeks he had grown used to having her in his home. He enjoyed her quiet yet decisive ways, her sense of humour and sharp intelligence. Sometimes she could be waspish, but he suspected her moods were caused through fear of consummating their marriage. If only he could break down her resistance! Julia was no ignorant Victorian miss, nor was she frigid—her response when he held her and kissed her told him that quite plainly.

Yet her awareness of what he felt for Erica obviously rankled in her mind. It was an attitude he could not understand, for she had married him knowing exactly how he felt. Could it be that Julia, like all women, wanted to be the first choice in her husband's life? She would never admit to being jealous, of course, but there was no other way to explain her behaviour.

Rising, Adam left the study and went upstairs to his bedroom. As he passed Julia's door he hesitated for a moment and then knocked.

'Yes?' she called.

'It's Adam,' he replied. 'I'd like to speak to you for a moment.'

After a few seconds she opened the door. She was

wearing a loose, flowing housecoat, and had washed off her make-up. She looked about sixteen—and a very innocent sixteen, at that.

'What do you want?' she asked.

'Only to say you can forget our bargain. Three months or three years won't make any difference to me. I'd never force myself on you no matter if we have to live like this for the rest of our lives.'

Her eyes widened and seemed to take on a deeper blue tinge. 'Thank you, Adam,' she said softly. 'I never expected you to say that, and I—I'm very touched.'

He stepped back. 'So now you can sleep well, without any nightmares of being forced into surrender.'

'They were never nightmares,' she murmured. 'I didn't mean to be so hurtful downstairs, but I lost my temper.'

'It's that red hair of yours,' he said ruefully. 'Beats me how you managed to control yourself when you were my secretary. There must have been many times when you longed to throw something at me.'

'Actually there weren't. I'm much more sensitive to your moods now than I ever was before.'

'The way a good wife should be,' Adam said dryly, and lifting his hand in a gesture of resignation, went to his room.

For many hours he lay sleepless; a rare occurrence with him, for he usually managed to blot out all his problems once he was in bed. Yet this problem was a personal one, which made it different. Restlessly he thumped his pillow. He had tried to resolve his unhappiness over Erica by taking a businesslike solution, and was beginning to see the inherent problems in it. Julia was seeing them too, as exemplified by her admission that she was far quicker-tempered with him now that he was her husband than she had been when he was her employer.

This meant their only hope of being happy together was for him to treat her as a friend and nothing more. He did not know how long he could maintain such a sexless attitude—he was a man, after all, not a monk—but he'd do his level best. Only in that way could he reassure Julia and hope—eventually—to break down the barrier she had erected between them.

'What a situation!' he muttered aloud. 'If I didn't like her so much I'd force her to surrender. Once she had, she'd soon see it was the best way for us to live.'

Yet he was mouthing words he had no intention of turning into action, and he accepted that for the foreseeable future, work was going to be his safety valve.

It was not a happy thought.

CHAPTER SEVEN

JULIA wondered why she wasn't relieved when Adam told her he wouldn't hold her to their bargain. After all, the prospect of physically becoming his wife had worried her since their wedding day. How illogical human beings were, she thought, slipping off her housecoat. When she had gone to Adam's room earlier this evening and asked him if he liked what she was wearing, she had sensed he was seeing her as a woman for the first time. She had realised then how it would feel to be Erica, the woman he really loved, and the knowledge that he was nonetheless willing to consummate a loveless marriage was something she had found infinitely degrading to herself.

Slipping on her nightdress, she glanced at the door. She had trusted Adam and never locked it, yet now she wanted to turn the key—which was ludicrous, considering he had just made a promise to leave her alone.

Her sleep that night was fitful and she dreamed about Adam and Erica, though she could only remember fragments of it when she awoke. Yet it left her with an awful feeling of rejection, and once again she was dismayed by the illogicality of her emotions. Though she called herself all kinds of a fool, her depression increased when Emilio told her Adam had a business dinner that night, and had left word he would not be home till late.

Reluctant to spend the evening on her own, Julia rang Susan Smith, who had taken her place at the office, and invited her to come over for a meal.

The girl accepted instantly, and at six-thirty was standing on the front doorstep. Julia had given the staff the evening off and opened the door herself, feeling less inhibited now she was alone.

'What a marvellous place!' Susan exclaimed, stepping into the hall, wide-eyed with curiosity. 'Somewhat different from your old homestead in Kentish Town.'

'You can say that again,' Julia grinned, having decided earlier in the day that false modesty was far more irritating than honest-to-goodness pleasure in her changed circumstances.

'I can't believe it's all yours,' Susan continued, stepping into the sitting room.

'It's Adam's,' Julia corrected.

'Yours as well now,' said Susan. 'You know the marriage vow: with all my worldly goods I thee endow?'

'How's life at the office?' Julia asked, deciding to change the subject.

'Much the same. We all miss you dreadfully. No one can argue with the boss the way you did.' Susan sat down. 'You look wonderful, Julia—like someone out of *Vogue*.'

'Thanks for the compliment, but I don't feel it.'

'Why not?'

'Because I'm bored. I'm not used to being a lady of leisure and I'm going potty looking for things to do.'

'You must be mad! If I were married to someone as rich as Adam, I'd wallow in doing nothing.'

'It's fine for a month or two,' Julia agreed. 'But after that it begins to pall.'

'Wait till you have a family. You'll soon find yourself hankering for days like this. Though I daresay you'll have a nanny to do all the chores.'

'If I had any children I'd look after them myself,' Julia replied, and turned quickly to the drinks tray.

'Just orange juice for me,' said Susan.

'I'll get some fresh orange from the kitchen.'

'Now you've disappointed me. I thought all you'd have to do was ring a bell and a genie would appear.'

'The genie and his wife are off for the evening,' Julia smiled. 'And so is the maid.'

'You mean we have to survive on our own?'

'Don't you think we're capable of it?'

Giggling, Susan followed Julia into the kitchen and watched as she took an orange from the vast American refrigerator and squeezed it through the electric juice extractor.

'How the rich live!' the girl sighed. 'This house has everything.'

Except a loving husband, Julia thought, and wondered what Susan would say if she knew. Yet she would never confide in Susan—or anyone else, for that matter. She owed Adam her loyalty and must pretend their marriage was a normal one.

'Can I carry anything through for you?' Susan asked.

'It's all set out on the table,' said Julia. 'We're just having something cold.'

'I like your use of the word "just",' Susan commented a little later as she surveyed the cantaloupe, salmon in dill sauce, and the sour cream and cucumber salad which accompanied it. 'I bet strawberries and cream come next.'

'Raspberries, actually, but I'm sure we have strawberries if you'd prefer.'

'Don't overdo it, dear friend, or I might come again!'

'I hope you will. I'm sorry Adam wasn't here to meet you.'

'I'm not. I don't think I'd have come if he'd been here. He wouldn't like it.'

'Don't be silly,' Julia said quickly. 'Adam's no snob. He may have faults, but that isn't one of them.'

'I know,' Susan agreed. 'And that wasn't what I meant. But you know how he likes to divide his life into compartments, and I don't think he'd find it easy to mix socially with members of his staff.'

'He married one,' Julia said dryly.

'Too true, but that doesn't negate what I said. He still likes to keep everybody and everything in separate sections. It's a form of rigidity.'

'Which is supposed to be a sign of insecurity,' Julia murmured, half to herself.

'Adam Lester insecure?' Susan was astounded. 'Only a woman who loved him would dare say a thing like that. You obviously see him in a different light from the rest of us.'

Julia dared not deny this, and silently offered Susan some salad; then started telling her about their trip to India, which was sufficiently interesting to take her friend's mind off Adam.

But later, when they had returned to the drawing room for coffee, Susan brought him into the conversation again.

'Don't you mind him going out and leaving you like this?' she asked.

'Why should I? He has to see clients and sometimes I'd be in the way.'

'Particularly when the client is Erica Dukes,' Susan said bluntly.

Julia's hands trembled and she put her cup on the table. Why hadn't Adam been truthful about tonight? She was aware of the younger girl eyeing her with ill-concealed curiosity and, angered by it, she gained strength.

'Adam has loads of women clients, and if I were jealous of them all my life would be hell.'

'Mrs Dukes was more than a client.'

'Which was what Adam wanted everyone to think.' It was hard for Julia to remain calm. 'It stopped everyone from guessing the truth about us.'

'Well, you succeeded on that score,' Susan said admiringly. 'I don't think it entered anyone's head that you and Adam were in love. Was your engagement to Roy also part of the whole thing?'

Julia hesitated, furious that she had not thought that Susan might ask such a question. She racked her brain trying to remember what she had said to the girl about it, and unable to recall, decided to go for the half-truth.

'I got engaged to Roy because I didn't think Adam

and I would ever marry.' At least that part of it was true. 'I knew he—that he loved me,' she continued quickly, 'but I couldn't see him actually settling down for years. So I decided to make a life for myself with Roy.'

'Which caused the green-eyed god of jealousy to erupt,' Susan giggled. 'So your little act paid off?'

'It seems like it,' Julia smiled. 'More coffee?'

'Yes, please.' Susan went over to look at the books on the shelves. 'Adam reads a lot, doesn't he? Islamic painting, Greek sculpture, travel books. I didn't know he had such wide interests. I always thought his sole interests were law—and beautiful women—until he married you, of course.'

Irritated by Susan's comments, Julia wished she had not invited her over. She feigned a yawn, then put her hand to her mouth.

'I'm afraid I'll have to ask you to go fairly soon,' she murmured. 'I had a very late night yesterday, and I can hardly keep my eyes open. It was our first dinner party,' she added, feeling an explanation was due. 'So I hope you'll forgive me for pushing you out.'

'Think nothing of it.' Susan helped herself to the last *petit four* on the tray. 'I've thoroughly enjoyed seeing you again, Julia. I wasn't sure if you'd be too grand to keep up with your old friends.'

Swallowing the retort that no one in the office had been particularly close to her, Julia smiled and rose. It had not been a good idea having Susan over, and she wouldn't repeat it. Sometimes circumstances changed a person too much for old situations to continue.

After Susan had left, Julia took the coffee cups down to the kitchen. Still unused to being waited on, she was reluctant to leave the dirty dishes for the maid, and washed them herself. She had almost finished when she heard a step behind her and turned to see Adam in the doorway.

'What are you doing?' he asked curtly.

'Washing the coffee things.'

'I pay staff to do that.'

'In a way, you pay me too.'

'I'm in no mood for smart answers, Julia.'

'Would you like a cup of coffee?' she asked, ignoring his comment.

'With honey to sweeten me, perhaps?'

'I doubt if honey is strong enough.'

A smile briefly touched his lips as he turned and went back into the hall. Drying her hands on a towel, Julia followed him into the library.

'I hope you had a nice evening?' she asked.

'No, I didn't. If you're not too tired, keep me company for a while. I'm in a foul temper.'

'Why?'

'I had dinner with Erica.' He paused, waiting. 'Surprised?' he asked into the silence.

'No. I knew it.'

'Been spying on me?'

'Of course.'

He looked up at this and then laughed. 'For a moment I almost believed you. But you're not the type to do such a thing, are you?'

Since the question seemed rhetorical, Julia let it pass. Adam stared silently into space and she waited, knowing he would eventually tell her what was worrying him. In the past, when she had been his secretary, he had often taken her into his confidence, appearing to enjoy her opinion even though he rarely took it. But this time the problem was Erica, and Julia was by no means sure she could give an unbiased opinion about her.

'Erica wants me to act for her,' he declared suddenly.

Julia was surprised. 'I thought you already did?'

'No. I used to handle her husband's affairs, but now she wants me to look after hers.'

'That will give you an excuse to see her.'

'I married *you* to stop seeing her.'

'Then refuse to act for her. It's a simple decision.'

'Except that if I refuse, she'll see it as a sign of weakness.'

'Still afraid of admitting to frailty, Adam?'

'Don't you be clever, too,' he said in a strangled voice, and jumped up.

Unfortunately Julia chose that moment to do the same, and they almost collided with one another. He reached out to steady her, his hands heavy on her shoulders.

'I thought you'd show some understanding, Julia, instead of mocking me.'

'You deserve to be mocked. You set yourself impossibly high standards and turn against people because they can't follow them.'

'I think there's a right and a wrong way to behave. *I've* always made a point of doing my best and——'

'Yet you married second best,' Julia interrupted. 'And it wasn't so terrible, was it?'

'It wasn't terrible at all,' he admitted. 'In fact it was the most sensible thing I ever did in my life.' His eyes roamed her face, his expression one of regret. 'Poor Julia, you have a way of making me feel a selfish swine.'

'You mean you're less than perfect?'

'Much less,' he said huskily, and pulling her close began to kiss her.

Julia smelled the brandy on his breath, and a sweeter, more cloying smell that could only have been Erica's scent. She tried to free herself, but Adam refused to release her, her struggles increasing his determination to make her respond. The pressure of his lips forced hers apart, and suddenly she was engulfed in a warmth that swept over her entire body like a tidal wave, battering at her defences and arousing her to a passion she could not control. Every part of her longed for his touch and her limbs trembled, so that she clung to him with all her strength, aching for him to dominate her reason as well as her body. Yet stubbornly her mind refused to succumb, and all she could think of was Erica, the woman from whom he had just come.

'Adam, stop it! Let me go!'

For an instant he took no notice, but as she began to struggle in his arms, he released her and stepped back.

'God!' he muttered in an angry voice. 'I always seem to be breaking my word to you. But I can't apologise for it this time. I'm not going to say I'm sorry I kissed you.'

'Why should you?' Julia asked stonily. 'You always use me as your whipping boy when Erica upsets you. She robs you of your confidence, so you come home and assert yourself with *me*.'

There was a noticeable change in the colour of Adam's face, and Julia wished she could retract what she had said.

'I'm sorry you feel that way about me,' he said tonelessly. 'I kissed you because you're beautiful and I wanted you. I can assured you I never thought of it in terms of asserting myself over you. Perhaps *you're* the one who should change,' he went on. 'Stop provoking me, and don't act as my mother figure.'

'Mother figure?' Julia was astounded.

'Well, you do love telling me what to do and where I'm going wrong,' he said dryly.

'Not any more,' Julia replied. 'From now on I'll stay on the sidelines and let you make your own mistakes.'

'I bet you won't.' Unexpectedly humour glinted in his eyes. 'You're too understanding, my dear. You'll always try to save me from myself.'

'Not from yourself,' she retorted, stung that he was so quickly in command of himself again. 'But from the Ericas of this world.'

'In the plural?'

'Of course. You're the type who'll always fall for that kind of woman.'

'Really?' he said dryly. 'I wonder why?'

'Because the Ericas of this world don't want a two-way

relationship—which would make demands on both parties. They only want sex and money. And you have plenty of both.'

'But not the ability to give anything else?' he asked bitterly. 'You have a very low opinion of my character, Julia. Thanks for telling me.'

Angrily he strode out, slamming the door behind him, and Julia stared after him in dismay, regretting her loss of temper. She usually kept her feelings under control, for the dramas of her childhood—her father's frequent disappearances and her mother's bitter weeping—had caused her to build up a defence against emotional involvement of any kind. It was true that because of this she might never reach the heights of ecstatic love, but neither would she sink into the abyss of total despair.

Now, however, she was being assailed by such irrational, violent emotions that she felt like a leaf tossed in a storm. She was furiously angry with Adam for being so weak where Erica was concerned, and equally angry with herself for caring. Yet wasn't it natural for her to have strong feelings about the situation? Though Adam had only married her to save face, he was nonetheless her husband and should stop dancing to Erica's tune.

Although she had no desire to apologise to him, she was too disturbed to sleep well—she had never had so many miserable nights in her life, she thought wryly—and awoke at six o'clock, unrefreshed and on edge. Slipping on a housecoat, she went down to the kitchen to make herself some coffee, and took it into the dining room. It was a room that showed up best at night, when the walls, covered in silk fabric, glowed richly under the candlelight, while the soft green curtains added satin lustre to the satinwood furniture and Tibetan rugs. But in the daytime the colours looked too sombre, and she stepped quickly through the french windows to the terrace leading to the long, narrow garden. She was still standing there, enjoying the sight of the flowering shrubs and colourful borders, when she heard Adam's step behind her. She would know it anywhere.

'Couldn't you sleep either, Julia?'

His drawn face was evidence that he too had had a restless night.

'I'm always awake early in summer,' she answered, unwilling to admit she had slept very little. 'If you prefer to eat breakfast alone, I can have it in my room.'

'Not at all. I like having you at the breakfast table.' He eyed her quizzically, making her aware of her vividly coloured housecoat, and her thick auburn hair all dishevelled.

'Gauguin would have loved to have painted you,' he said softly. 'Even I get an urge to try.'

'I didn't know you painted.'

'I'm what's known as a Sunday amateur.'

She smiled. 'I can't imagine you being amateur at anything.'

'You have greater faith in my ability than I have—and that's saying something!'

Before she could reply, he placed a finger over her lips. 'Let's stop teasing each other, shall we? Or at least call a truce until noon each day.'

'I wasn't teasing you. I meant every word.' Julia went back into the dining room with him, making a slight face as she glanced over her shoulder at the garden. 'I wish it was always warm enough to breakfast *al fresco*,' she commented. 'This room's too dark to use so early in the day.'

'There's a small one on the side of this,' he said. 'You could turn it into a breakfast room if you wish. At the moment I only use it for storing things.'

'I'd like to see it.' She looked about her but could see no other door. 'Where did you say it was?'

'Behind you,' Adam pointed. 'The lock is covered by the wall covering. You have to press firmly on one particular spot.'

'A secret room!' she exclaimed, running eagerly towards the wall. 'How fascinating!'

'To the right of you,' said Adam as she pressed vainly on the wall. 'A bit higher, Julia. Where you can see faint mark on the fabric.'

Julia tried again. There was a click and a narrow door swung back to reveal a room about seven feet square. It was choc-à-bloc with cases and books, and a tiny window looked out on the garden.

'It would make a perfect breakfast room,' she said excitedly.

'Then regard it as yours.' Adam helped himself to bacon and eggs. 'You can do what you like with it.'

'Really?'

'That's what I said. As long as you don't bother me with any of the details.'

Somewhat chilled by this, Julia returned to the dining room table and sat down. 'I'm surprised you show so little interest in your home.'

'I used to be extremely interested when I——' He stopped, embarrassed.

'There's no need to look apologetic,' said Julia. 'I realise that living here with me is different from what it would have been with Erica.'

'It was tactless of me to say so.'

'Truth usually has a habit of revealing itself.'

'Sometimes too late,' he said dryly.

Julia guessed he was still referring to Erica, and knew there was no way she could sweeten the bitterness of his thoughts.

'I'm thrilled about the little room,' she said impulsively. 'I can't wait to start on it. I'll make it bright but cosy.'

'You'll be wanting a cat and a canary next.'

'I'd love a cat,' Julia confessed.

Half expecting Adam to say she could have one, she was disappointed when he made no comment, and shortly afterwards he pushed back his chair. 'I'm afraid I'll be dining out again tonight, Julia. I meant to tell you last evening, but it slipped my mind.'

Julia immediately envisaged him with Erica, and watched silently as he went to the door. On the threshold he turned to her.

'I'm not dining with Erica, if that's what you think. I'll be with an American client who's just flown in from San Francisco. He wants to talk privately to me about something, otherwise I'd have asked him to come here.'

Julia tried not to show she was pleased he had bothered to give her an explanation. 'I may go to a concert,' she said. 'There's something good on at the Festival Hall.'

'I didn't know you liked music.'

'There's a lot you don't know about me.'

'I'll have to start learning.'

'Like a good husband?' she asked wryly.

'If something's worth doing, it's worth doing well.' Adam hesitated. 'I know I've said all this before, but when I asked you to marry me I knew it wasn't going to be easy for either of us. But we're both intelligent people and if we try to make a go of it, I'm sure we'll succeed. But it has to be a joint effort.'

'I *am* trying, Adam.'

'Implying that I'm not?'

'How can I speak for you?'

'You don't need to,' he said. 'The look on your face is enough!'

After Adam left, Julia went back into the little adjoining room. She had a fair idea of what she wanted to do here. First she would have French doors leading out on to the terrace, then she would make the room look like an extension of the garden, with trellis wallpaper, cane furniture and an abundance of plants. There should also be a gaily tiled floor, with tablecloth and matching chair covers, preferably in a flowery print. She could see it in her mind's eye already: warm, colourful, gay. But first she must find a builder.

After she had dressed, Julia spent the rest of the morning on the telephone, and by midday found a contractor who agreed to come to inspect the room and give her a quote that very hour.

'There's a delay in the job I'm doing at present,' he explained when he saw her. 'So if it suits you, I could start work tomorrow. With any luck we should finish by the end of the week.'

This was far quicker than Julia had anticipated, but she was careful to hide her pleasure in case the price went up, and only when they had agreed a fee did she let her enthusiasm show.

By four o'clock that afternoon, Julia had found the furniture she wanted. It was in a little shop off Sloane Street, which also stocked curtain materials.

'We can do tablecloths and napkins too,' the proprietress said. 'Why don't we pick out the three main colours in the curtaining and have a set made in each shade, with white trimmings to match the cane.'

'That sounds super,' Julia enthused, and left the shop too keyed up to go straight home. Instead, she wandered into Hyde Park, doing her best to ignore the constant stream of traffic rushing past her.

Not even the fume-filled air could dim the beauty of the trees nor the lushness of the emerald grass, which looked well washed by the recent rains. The roses were already unfolding their petals and displaying their full beauty, like women ready for love. It was a fanciful notion and she was annoyed for having thought it. Marriage was changing her more than she had anticipated, and Adam was occupying far too much of her attention.

Leaving the park, she made her way to Chester Street. How the day had flown; there was nothing better than being busy, to make time speed by. She really must do something about finding a job, even if it was only part-time. Adam didn't want her to return to the office, but there were plenty of other legal practices, and if he disapproved of her working for a rival firm, she would try an entirely new field. Perhaps with an interior decorator. It might be interesting and fun.

The first thing Julia noticed as she let herself into the hall was a small wicker basket on the floor. She frowned at it, and was about to move forward for a closer look, when it creaked loudly. With a gasp of fright she jumped back. Then she heard a tiny plaintive miaow and saw a small grey paw emerge through the side of the basket.

'It arrived for you this afternoon, madam,' Emilio told her, coming into the hall. 'There was a note with it, which I put on the table.'

Julia picked up the envelope and took out the card. The message was in Adam's hand: 'While you're training this little minx to hold in its claws, perhaps you'll learn to do the same yourself!'

Amused, she put the card in her pocket, then lifted the cover of the basket. A small white kitten with large green eyes stared up at her.

'Oh, you darling!' she exclaimed, cradling it in her arms. Its fur was thick as a Persian's, and snow white, except for dark grey ears, fat paws and a large bushy tail, also grey. 'You're beautiful,' she breathed. 'And very unusual. I wonder what breed you are?'

'There were some instructions inside the basket,' said Emilio. 'Perhaps they may tell you.'

Hurriedly she scanned the printed foolscap sheet he handed her. 'It's a Burmese,' she explained. 'They're holy cats that used to live in Buddhist temples, and are supposed to be of royal lineage.'

Emilio chuckled. 'Well, she looks like a princess. Does she have a name?'

'According to her pedigree, it's something quite unpronounceable. But I think you've already named her.'

'I have?' The butler's usually impassive features were alight with surprise.

'You said she looks like a princess, so that's what we'll call her.'

Beaming at the news, Emilio went into the kitchen to tell his wife, while Julia, hugging the kitten close, went into the drawing room. She would have to buy a litter tray and some food. Probably milk and scraps would do for this evening.

At last she knew why Adam had not reacted this morning when she had said she would love a cat. He had obviously decided there and then to get her one. She was extremely touched by his thoughtfulness, and realised again how much she still had to learn about him.

'Perhaps *you'll* help me to get to know him better, Princess,' she whispered against the silky fur, and the kitten's contented purr seemed a good omen for the future.

CHAPTER EIGHT

THE breakfast room was completed in just over a week. Julia managed to keep it a surprise for Adam by ensuring that the builder arrived and left while he was away from the house, so that there was no sign of activity or mess.

On the morning it was finally ready for use, she was up at seven to supervise the laying of the table and to make sure everything looked its best: the white cane furniture, whose green upholstery was dotted with gay sprigs of flowers that matched the fabric hanging on the walls; the terracotta tiled floor and the rustic-looking French windows opening to the terrace. Happily she gazed about her. She could have been in a little dining room in the heart of the Mediterranean, rather than in fume-filled London. She only hoped Adam would like it as much as she did.

She was on her second cup of coffee when she heard him enter the dining room. He paused as he saw the dining table was unlaid, then noticing that the secret door was open, he came through it.

'Good God!' he exclaimed in astonishment. 'You've worked a minor miracle here, Julia—congratulations! This is just what a breakfast room should be like. And you've co-ordinated everything perfectly too.' He smiled at her. 'A beautiful picture in an elegant frame.'

'Compliments at eight-thirty in the morning? You must be in a wonderful mood!'

'You shouldn't sound so surprised. I always used to be—when you were my secretary.'

Julia made a face at him. 'Perhaps you're a better employer than a husband!'

He chuckled, in no way put out by her comment,

though the answer he gave showed that he had taken it seriously.

'A business relationship is easier to maintain than a personal one, Julia. As I think we're both beginning to realise. Though I must say my feelings towards Susan Smith occasionally verge on the murderous! She never stops moaning and bursts into tears at the slightest provocation.'

'Then you'll have to be more careful with her,' Julia said firmly. 'You have a quick mind and a razor-sharp tongue, which can be really petrifying.'

'It never petrified you.'

Accepting this, Julia frowned. 'If you're not satisfied with Susan, I'll be happy to find someone else for you.'

Adam looked about to say yes, then shook his head. 'You're my wife, Julia. I don't want you getting your roles mixed.'

Crossing over to the hotplate on the bamboo trolley, he helped himself to some grilled kidneys and bacon before sitting at the table, taking a chair that gave him a view of the terrace and garden.

'This is considerably nicer than the other dining room,' he said. 'I feel as if I'm in the country.'

'I'm surprised you don't have a place out of town.'

'This was enough for me to cope with when I was on my own. But it might be worth considering now. Perhaps you'd like to start looking around?'

'Don't buy anything just because I suggested it,' Julia said hastily.

'You know me better than that. I never do anything unless I really want to. No, I think we should have a second house. And a good-sized one, too.'

Julia guessed he was thinking of the future and the family he hoped to have, and she felt herself blushing. To hide her embarrassment, she bent and picked up Princess and placed her on her lap.

'What part of the country would you like?' she asked evenly.

'Somewhere not more than an hour's drive from London, and on a motorway.'

'Houses like that are expensive.'

'I work hard in order to afford expensive things,' he replied, and mentioned a price range that took her breath away. 'Just because Erica didn't find me rich enough, it doesn't mean I'm a pauper.'

'I'll start contacting the estate agents today,' Julia said stiltedly. 'But don't expect as quick a result as we had with the breakfast room.'

'I won't. Take your time with it, my dear. Finding a house and furnishing it should be an interesting occupation for you.'

'To keep me busy till we can furnish it with babies,' she said tartly.

His lips tightened. 'I promised I wouldn't keep you to our bargain, but we'll never have a chance of happiness if you're constantly on the defensive with me.'

'I know,' she sighed. 'But has it crossed your mind that even if we eventually have a normal marriage, I mightn't be able to have children?'

'Or perhaps *I* cannot,' he answered quietly. 'But if that were the case, we'd adopt.'

'You think of everything.'

'It's part of my training.' He glanced at his watch. 'I must be off. I've a busy day ahead of me, and I'm afraid I'm out to dinner again tonight.'

'That will be the fourth time in a fortnight!' she exclaimed.

'I know, and I'm terribly sorry. I've made a vow that from now on I'll only dine out if it's really urgent. I feel guilty at leaving you so much on your own.'

'I'm beginning to think it's what you prefer.'

Adam rose and came over to her, placing his hand beneath her chin. 'I like being with you, Julia—more than

I can tell you. But some clients only have time to see me in the evenings, and I've always given in to them. But from now on I won't do it—even if I lose them.'

'Don't lose any clients on my account,' she answered. 'I shouldn't have said anything to you, Adam. I'm sorry.'

'I'm not. I'm glad you did.' His hand dropped from her chin to rest on her shoulder. 'Treat me as you would a real husband, Julia. It's what I want.' Swiftly he bent and pressed his mouth to the soft skin at the side of her throat. 'You smell delicious,' he whispered, then straightened and walked out.

The feel of Adam's mouth on her skin lingered long after he had gone, and Julia was vaguely disturbed by it. Living with Adam was like sitting on a see-saw—one moment up and the next down. The only certain thing was that she could not get off. She was Adam's wife and had committed herself to him. But what would happen after four years when Erica inherited Kenneth's money and was free to remarry? Would she still want Adam and, more important, would he still want her? He maintained that he wouldn't, and to prove it had made a loveless marriage. But he might well feel differently when the time came to actually make a choice, particularly once Erica was free to pressurise him.

Despondently Julia returned to her bedroom. What could she do with herself today, now that the breakfast room was finished?' A few phone calls to estate agents, perhaps, and then some shopping. If only she had a job. When she had been obliged to go to the office every day she had hankered for a time of limitless leisure, but now all she longed for was the opportunity to work.

At ten o'clock she wandered across to the boutique in Sloane Street, where she had bought some clothes a few weeks previously. The owner was already in and she tried on several outfits and bought three, not batting an eyelid when the bill came to more than she would have spent on clothes in a year, when she was single. I'm developing the mentality of the idle rich, she thought wryly as she left the shop. The idle and discontented rich.

Lunching at the snack counter at Fortnum & Masons, she passed an hour studying everyone around her. Elegant, middle-aged women were talking in loud upper-class voices to their friends and daughters; the girls being mostly of an awkward age, obviously having left the class-room recently. A few were dressed in way-out clothes, with hair to match, but even they spoke in the same ring-ing tones as their mothers.

Feeling like a fish out of water, Julia was glad to escape to the bustle of Bond Street, where she eventually gravit-ated to the beautifully filled windows of Aspreys. This was where the rich sheiks from Saudi Arabia and the Gulf States did their shopping, buying thousand-pound watches as carelessly as if they were Woolworth trinkets. As she eyed a lavish alligator and gold weekend case, its interior fitted with real gold-capped bottles, she became aware of the reflection of a man in the window pane. He was looking at her and she half turned, astonished to see Roy.

'I thought it was you,' he stammered, a pink flush marking his pale skin. 'I rang you at your office this morning, but the switchboard said you'd left, and I was going to call you at home this evening.'

'You wouldn't have found me there, either,' she replied. 'I moved three months ago.'

Although she was managing to talk with composure, Julia was shocked by her encounter with him, and wondered why he looked so different from the way she remembered: he was shorter and thinner; almost weedy when compared with the broad-shouldered Adam.

'I thought you were in Canada,' she went on.

'I came back two days ago. Things didn't work out and my firm decided they wanted me in London.' Roy avoided Julia's eyes. 'My engagement didn't work out either, which is why I wanted to see you. I was a fool, Julia. I don't know how I could have behaved the way I did. It was inexcusable, so I won't bother trying to defend it, but I've come to my senses now and I'll do everything in my power to get you back.'

Julia heard Roy out, though it was as if she were listening to a stranger. Could this thin, pale-faced man be the one she had loved so desperately a bare few months ago? It seemed incredible, yet she knew it was.

'Say it isn't too late for us,' he pleaded. 'I'll understand if you don't want to get engaged to me yet, but if you'll let me see you, perhaps in time . . .'

'I'm afraid not,' Julia said quietly, holding out her hand to show him her wedding ring. 'It's too late, Roy.'

Stupefied, he stared at it.

'It didn't take you long to find someone else,' he said finally, in a choked voice.

'Longer than it took *you*.'

He had the grace to look ashamed. 'I deserved that, Julia. I suppose you must hate me?'

Julia shook her head. 'Hating someone takes up too much of one's energy. Besides, it's pointless for us to be enemies.'

'I was my own worst enemy,' he admitted. 'Letting you go was the most crassly stupid thing I've done in my life.' He hesitated. 'I wish I could go on talking to you, but I'm already late for an appointment with my chairman. I don't suppose there's any chance of us meeting?'

'I'm at a loose end tonight, as it so happens. My husband has a business dinner.' Even as she spoke, Julia wondered why she had agreed to his suggestion. But it was too late to go back on it, for Roy looked delighted.

'That's great! Really great. If you give me your address I'll come and collect you.'

'It might be better if we met at Carlo's,' she said, naming an Italian restaurant where they had frequently eaten. 'Is eight o'clock all right?'

'I'll be counting the hours,' Roy replied, and dashed across the road to grab a vacant taxi.

Julia turned back to Aspreys' window, but she was no longer in the mood to look at luxury trifles and decided to return home. -

Relaxing in the bath, she was assailed by guilt for having agreed to meet Roy, and forcefully reminded herself that Adam had no compunction about going out with Erica. It was this knowledge which spurred her into wearing an elegant black chiffon dress instead of the casual crêpe she had earlier decided on. After all, why shouldn't she look her best when dining with her ex-fiancé? And if Adam saw her when she returned home, so much the better.

She arrived at Carlo's shortly after the agreed hour to find Roy already waiting at a table. He too had taken pains to look his best, and his light grey suit, obviously American in its styling, made him look much more attractive than the usual dark conservative clothes he favoured. Yet he still didn't compare with Adam. Damn it, she thought angrily, I've got to stop thinking of that man.

'I was half afraid you'd change your mind,' Roy smiled, pulling out a chair for her.

'I nearly did,' she confessed. 'But then it seemed silly.'

'I'd have understood. I acted like a swine and I know it.'

'It still didn't stop you from doing it,' she said dryly, and seeing him colour, knew they couldn't go on raking over the past. 'Let's not talk about what happened,' she continued briskly. 'If we do, I'll only say something hurtful.'

'Is that because you still care for me?'

'Not at all. I have no feelings for you whatever.'

Her answer came out spontaneously, and only as it did did Julia realise exactly how she felt about Roy. She didn't love him, and with hindsight she knew she never had. What on earth could she have seen in this precise, pedantic man, with his fussy ways and narrow outlook?

'I appreciate why you're saying this, Julia,' Roy spoke stiffly, 'but I don't believe it. One doesn't stop loving someone merely because one wants to. I'm not being smug, my dear, but I'm pretty sure you married on the rebound.'

'Much as I don't want to disappoint you, I'm afraid you're wrong. Soon after you jilted me, I realised that what I'd felt for you would never have been strong enough for us to have had a successful marriage.'

'You were willing to become my wife.'

'Only because I was running away from deeper feelings.'

'And you aren't any more?'

'No.'

'What made you stop?'

'I'm not sure,' Julia said slowly.

'Who's the lucky man you *did* marry?' Roy asked in hurt tones. 'It's quite obvious you've fallen in love with him.'

Julia almost told him she was in love with no one, until she remembered Adam's desire for everyone to believe their marriage was normal, so she shrugged and said casually: 'Adam Lester.'

'Adam Lester!' Roy's voice was so loud with astonishment that people at the surrounding tables stared at them. 'Adam Lester,' he repeated, lowering his voice. 'Now I see why you forgot me so quickly! I bet you were in love with him all along.'

Again Julia wondered whether to tell him the truth about her marriage, but decided against it.

'When did you discover he was in love with *you*?' Roy demanded.

'One can't always pinpoint the exact moment of falling in love,' she hedged. 'You should know that. Let's just say it happened.'

'Does he know about me?'

'Of course. It was when he discovered you'd jilted me

that he started seeing me as a woman instead of simply his secretary.'

'You mean I've only myself to blame? Oh, Julia, what a fool I've been! You're more beautiful than ever. Different, too.' His glance took in the stylish cut of her dress, from which her satin-smooth shoulders rose. 'More beautiful than ever,' he repeated. 'And I still love you.'

'Then you should stop.' Julia marvelled she could be so unmoved by his declaration. 'I'm married now and I'm not looking for any intrigues.'

'Nor am I,' he said swiftly. 'I'm not the type.'

This was so true that Julia nearly laughed. 'Tell me about Toronto,' she said quickly. 'And why your love affair went wrong.'

'She wasn't the girl I thought. At first she seemed everything I'd dreamed of—pretty, gentle, quiet. But she soon turned from Jekyll into Hyde. With you, it was the reverse. You look exotic and demanding but you're really the most docile of girls.'

'I'm not sure I find that particularly flattering,' Julia smiled. 'Although I know you mean it as a compliment.'

Roy looked somewhat put out, but did not argue. 'Tell me about yourself,' he said instead. 'I take it you've no regrets?'

'What a question to ask a newly married woman! Of course I haven't. I couldn't be happier.'

Once again Roy looked hurt, but he regained his self-control and started to tell her about his life and work in Canada. He had never been a scintillating conversationalist, but when talking about business he had a serious and intelligent point of view, and managed to hold Julia's interest for several hours.

With a start she realised it was after eleven o'clock and hurriedly pushed back her chair. 'I'd better be going, or Adam will wonder where I am.'

'I won't ask if I can see you again,' Roy murmured a little later as he stopped the car outside the house in

Chester Street. 'But if you'd like us to meet, you know where to find me.'

'Don't stay in for my call.' She smiled to take the sting out of her reply. 'It might be better if we didn't see one another again—better for you, I mean.'

'I doubt that.' He got out of the car and accompanied her to the front door. 'I'm feeling very sorry for myself right now, but if you're happy in your marriage, then I'm delighted for you.' Leaning forward, he kissed her on the cheek. 'Take care of yourself—and don't forget I'm always available if you need me.'

Julia let herself into the hall. It was in darkness except for a light which made a small pool of radiance on the staircase. Careful not to make a noise, she went up to her room and quietly closed the door. Almost at once there was a loud rap on it, and with heart beating fast, she opened it again.

Adam glared down at her from the threshold, his dark red dressing gown making him look slightly sinister, as did the icy glitter in his eyes.

'Where have you been?' he demanded.

'Out to dinner with a friend. A man,' she added.

'Couldn't you have left word with Emilio? I've been waiting up for you for hours.' Adam's eyes moved involuntarily towards the window and she guessed he had seen her arrive home.

'Spying on me?' she asked frigidly.

'You weren't in when I got back, so when I heard a car draw up, I naturally looked out to see if it was you. It was late and I was worried.'

'It's not yet midnight. But thanks for being concerned.'

'Who was it?' he asked.

'Roy. My—the man I was supposed to marry.'

'You mean the one who jilted you to marry someone else?'

'He didn't in the end. Things went wrong for him and he returned to England.'

'And no doubt would like to return to you? Is that why you went out with him—because you still fancy him?'

'Don't be silly, Adam—I bumped into him in Bond Street at lunchtime today, and he asked if he could see me again. As I was free tonight . . .'

'You didn't waste much time, did you?'

'Would you rather I'd stayed in by myself?'

'You're damn right I would!'

Stung by Adam's tone, Julia felt her temper rise. 'There was no harm in my going out with Roy. You're being ridiculously old-fashioned!'

'Because I object to my bride being seen out with another man?'

So that was why he was angry. Adam didn't really mind her seeing Roy. What he objected to was other people seeing it. His damn pride again!

'Next time I'll have dinner with him in his flat,' she said icily. 'Then we won't be seen and your pride won't be hurt.'

'I've no intention of allowing you to see him again *anywhere*,' he snapped. 'You're my wife and you'll behave as such.'

'You're being absurd. I suggest you go to bed and that we talk about it tomorrow, when you're less tired.'

'Don't dismiss me as if I'm a child!' Adam came further into the room, but Julia ignored him and, turning to the dressing table, took off her earrings and then went into the bathroom.

Hearing no further sound from the bedroom, she assumed he had left, and with trembling fingers she undressed, put on her nightdress and returned to the bedroom. Only then did she see Adam still standing there.

'I want to talk about Roy *tonight*, Julia, not tomorrow.' His voice was clipped. 'I'm not giving you time to think up some excuse for seeing him.'

'I don't need an excuse,' she said angrily, reaching for her dressing gown. 'I told you why I saw Roy, so stop looking at me as though I'm a fallen woman!'

'I'm looking at my wife,' Adam said harshly. 'Do you know what time I came home tonight? Ten o'clock. And I brought Frank Carter with me, too.'

'Frank Carter?'

'The client with whom I had dinner. I wanted him to meet you. You can imagine how I felt when Emilio told me you were dining out. I had to pretend I'd forgotten.'

'I was going to a concert anyway, remember? But I don't see why you needed to pretend you hadn't remembered. I'm not in purdah, and if I'm left alone and I want to go out, I will.'

'Not with other men, though. I won't stand for that.'

Knowing Adam's temperament, Julia could appreciate why he was angry. It must have been embarrassing in the extreme, to bring a client home to meet his loving bride and find her absent from the nest.

'The whole thing was just unfortunate,' she said in a placatory tone. 'I'm sure Mr Carter won't think you're a cuckolded husband, because I wasn't here to welcome him.'

'That remark is in very poor taste,' Adam snapped. 'And why make it anyway? Or is that what you and your ex-fiancé intend making of me?'

Julia's smile held more than a hint of sarcasm. 'Be careful what you say, Adam, or I may think you're jealous.'

'That's exactly what I am! You're my wife and I won't let anyone else have you. One woman has already made a fool of me, and it's not going to happen again.'

With a swift movement he stepped forward and caught her by the arms. Before she could even try to break away, he pushed her up against the bed.

'You belong to me,' he grated. 'Is my message clear, or do I have to show you what I mean?'

'You don't have to show me anything. Just say what you want to say and get out of my room.'

'Not yet. I'll go when I'm ready and not a minute before.'

Angered by his reply, Julia kicked at his shins. He gave a muttered imprecation and then gripped her so hard that she was powerless to move.

'You're mine,' he grated. 'Do you understand that? Mine, and I won't let you go!'

Wildly he began to kiss her—hard, angry kisses, as if trying to brand her. Julia's skin was rasped by his abrasive touch and she struggled to free herself.

'Let me go!' she cried. 'You're hurting me!'

But her words inflamed him the more and he pushed her on to the bed and fell upon her, the weight of his body pinning her down.

'I've been waiting for you for almost two hours,' he muttered, his breath warm upon her mouth. 'Wondering where you were, who you were with ... My God, you don't know what you've done to me!'

All too clearly Julia was beginning to realise, and as she did, her anxiety grew. She had to get Adam away from her before he became completely uncontrollable. But this was easier said than done, for as she tried to inch her body out from under his, he felt the movement and instantly tightened his hold.

'No, you don't,' he said thickly. 'You're not escaping from me this time. I'm tired of being played for a fool— first Erica and now you. But not any more. From now on, *I'll* call the tune.'

Julia gazed up at him. It was like looking at a stranger. Adam's eyes were narrow slits and his hair was dishevelled. A vein stood out on his temple, giving him a vulnerable air that made her feel unexpectedly sorry for him. Poor Adam! How he must have tormented himself in these last few hours.

'I want you, Julia,' he whispered against her throat. 'Don't turn me away, darling. Not tonight.'

His hands moved over her body and his chest pressed

into hers, crushing her breasts. His breathing was fast, as if he had been running or fighting. Yes, fighting was the better word, for he had been fighting for self-control and had lost the battle, as Julia was losing hers. Yet she no longer cared. All she wanted to do was obliterate the hurt in Adam's eyes; the anguish he was experiencing because of his belief that she was going to let him down the way Erica had. How blind he was not to see she wanted to protect him; that she loved him too much to let him be hurt all over again.

The enormity of what she had just admitted drove everything else from her mind. Surely it couldn't be true? Yet she knew it was. Love had overtaken her while she was not looking; growing out of propinquity perhaps, but nonetheless there. Yet pride forbade her from letting Adam know. He wanted succour, not love; intelligent interest rather than blatant desire. To know she loved him would place a burden of guilt upon him that only his reciprocation of her love could remove, and since he wasn't able to reciprocate, she dared not let him guess her feelings. Tears flooded her eyes and spilled down her cheeks, and noticing the moisture on his skin, Adam lessened the fierceness of his hold and raised himself slightly to look into her face.

'Don't be scared of me, Julia,' he said softly. 'But we can't go on as we are. You're a beautiful, desirable woman and it isn't possible for me to live with you and not want you. That's why I was so furious with you tonight. You were right when you said I was jealous, and I can't deny it any longer.'

He started kissing her again, and though it would have been all too easy to respond to his touch, the knowledge that she was still an object to him—albeit an object of desire—made her unwilling to surrender. Yet her body played traitor to her mind, and his gently roaming hands were wreaking havoc with her firm intentions.

'I won't hurt you,' he murmured huskily, clasping her

face in his hands and looking down at her with passionate intensity. 'You're my wife, Julia, and once we're physically close, we won't be so on edge with each other.'

'No!' she cried. 'I don't want you to——'

But the rest of what she was going to say was obliterated by the pressure of his mouth on hers, while the subtle exploration of his hands, so sensitive to every part of her body, was her total undoing. Desire scorched through her like a flame and she could no longer resist him. She ached with the need to be taken and by him—only him—and like an empty vessel she longed for him to fill her with the seed of his love. For it *was* a kind of love, she told herself. Not the all-consuming madness he felt for Erica, but a steadier, more realistic emotion that might one day blossom into something more.

'I love you,' she whispered, but his kisses muffled her words and he did not hear them. They came together without a sound, either from him or from her.

CHAPTER NINE

ADAM opened his eyes and stared at the cream silk curtains through which the early morning light was filtering.

Cream silk? But his were blue. With a startled movement he sat up. Where the hell was he? Then he remembered. Turning his head, he looked at the sleeping figure beside him. Julia, his wife. The woman he had taken against her will.

With a stifled groan he buried his head in his hands, wishing he could turn back the clock twenty-four hours. But it was impossible, and he knew that for the rest of his life he would have to live with the memory of what he had done. How could he have acted in such a way? How could insane jealousy have goaded him into using force to take a woman?

Of course he had wanted Julia for a long time. At first he had thought it was the natural desire of a man to possess a beautiful girl. But of late he had begun to realise the attraction was more than physical. He enjoyed talking to her, he respected her opinions, he appreciated her sense of humour. In short—and he might as well admit it— he loved her. Loved her with a depth he had never experienced for anyone else, a depth that made his feelings for Erica shallow and paltry.

Carefully he shifted his position so that he could study Julia more carefully. Her dark red tresses were splayed across the pillow, her skin was creamy as a magnolia bud and had the sheen of a pearl, and the movement of her breasts as she stirred and shifted on the pillow made him long to rest his face against their warm softness. He bent closer to her. Her incredibly long lashes rested upon her cheeks in two dark crescents, and her lips were slightly

parted to show the faint gleam of her teeth. In sleep she
was totally relaxed and her face, devoid of its usual
guarded expression, looked infinitely young and vulnerable, making him realise how carefully she had disguised
her feelings and her real self.

He ached to hold her close, to feel once more the softness of her body against his own, and the silky smoothness
of her skin beneath his hands. But for the moment passion
was spent, though he knew it would not remain so if he
went on looking at her.

But guilt overrode his growing desire, and he got swiftly
out of bed and went to his room. Slipping a dressing gown
over his naked body, he sat in a chair and stared morosely
through the window, too preoccupied with his thoughts
to heed the view or hear the chorus of the birds. Again he
cursed himself for having been so aggressive and insensitive, and sought comfort from the fact that all he had
wanted was to prove to himself and Julia that having a
genuine marriage—physical as well as mental closeness—
was the only way to make their future life together a
happy one.

Although he had only married to save face, he had
soon seen Julia for what she was worth, and not simply as
a sop to his vanity. Their trip to India had been one of
the most enjoyable holidays of his life, for she had not
only proved an attractive, charming companion, but an
intelligent one. What a crass idiot he had been not to let
her know his feelings towards her were changing!

And then last night things had come to a head. Arriving
home with Frank Carter, he had been furious not to find
her waiting for him. Reason had told him that if *he* went
out in the evening, she had every right to do the same;
and to be fair she had warned him she might be going to
a concert. But unexpectedly for him, emotion had over-
ridden reason and, like a jealous lover, he had waited for
her return. After what seemed an eternity she had finally
arrived, accompanied by a man who had had the nerve

to˙kiss her goodnight at the front door. His front door. The rage that had welled up in Adam had been uncontrollable. Once more a woman was making a fool of him.

As soon as Julia reached her room he had barged into it, and the sight of her in a black dress that showed every curve of her body had inflamed him to such passion that he had determined no man other than himself would ever have her.

'You're mine!' he had ground out, and had used his strength to overcome her and prove it.

But what—in the cold light of the following dawn—had he actually proved? He had taken Julia, yet he did not feel any closer to her. On the contrary, he felt more of a stranger. Was it because he had sensed her fear of him? For a fleeting moment he had had the impression that she wanted to respond, but it had been so momentary, and had so quickly changed to mute acquiescence, that he had felt he was making love to a doll. Yet Julia was a flesh and blood woman and one day she would admit it to him. But she wouldn't do it yet. First he had to gain her trust, which wasn't going to be easy; he had to make her believe he bitterly regretted forcing her into submission. The act of love should be a mutual giving and taking, rising together to the heights of ecstasy and a gradual, mutual descent, with tenderness taking over from passion. But there had been nothing like this between himself and Julia. Only his own passion and release. She had given nothing of herself and, because of it, his victory had been bitter.

Dressing hurriedly, Adam went downstairs. As he passed Julia's door, he paused, then turned the handle and went in. She was still asleep, her arms outstretched on the pillow. She wore no nightdress and a silken fold of the sheet rested against the curve of her breasts. He longed to kiss them but knew he dared not. He had vowed there would be no repeat of last night. Not until she believed he

genuinely loved her would he show her his desire. Yet
how would she react if he told her he no longer loved
Erica, but herself? What proof could he give that his
feelings were lasting?

He wondered when his doubts about Erica had begun.
He had realised from the start that marriage to her would
never be easy—she was too quick-tempered and self-
centred. But then so was he. Indeed his very egocentricity
had kept him from admitting earlier on what his true
feelings for Erica were. To admit to an error of judgment
was a recognition of failure, and failure had always been
anathema to him—a fact which Julia knew and despised.
In the same way that she knew why he had married her.
Except that now his reasons were totally different. Julia
was the one woman he wanted to protect and cherish; the
one person with whom he knew he could find oneness of
spirit and peace.

Peace. It was a long while since he had dreamed of
finding this with anyone. In his previous estimation, peace
had been the conclusion of a successful court case; more
security in the bank; another directorship. He had never
even thought to achieve it with Erica, which showed what
a damn fool he was. Yet not such a fool as not to see what
Julia had come to mean to him.

Julia, who had quietly infiltrated his very being. Who
had moved into his house and made it a home.

She stirred on the pillows and opened her eyes, and he
stepped back quickly. But it was too late: she had seen
him. Blushing, she sat up, pulling the sheets over her
naked body.

'Good morning,' he said weakly. 'I—I've been watching you. I want to . . . I'd like to talk to you.'

'Don't you think your actions last night said
enough?'

'Too much, perhaps—which is why I beg you to forgive
me.'

'So you can go on living with an easy conscience?' she

retorted. 'Well, you'll have to do it without my for-giveness.'

'I thought you'd say that,' he said huskily. 'But couldn't you at least show some understanding as to why it happened?'

'What understanding have you ever shown *me*?' Julia questioned.

Her eyes—in their anger—were blue as delphiniums, her tousled hair an aureole of wine flame around her head. Never had she looked more desirable, nor regarded Adam with greater dislike. Short of kneeling at her feet and tell-ing her exactly how he felt, he didn't know what to do. Yet even if he confessed the truth, she would doubt him. Only time would make her accept that he meant every word. Time, and the way he behaved towards her during the next few months.

Hiding his anguish, he said calmly: 'More than any-thing, I want us to have a normal marriage. I know I promised I wouldn't force you into a physical relationship, and that last night I broke my word, but there were ex-tenuating circumstances, which I realise you're still too upset to see. However, I beg you not to let it spoil our future.'

'A future of what?' Julia asked. 'Of forcing me to submit to you?'

'I'll never use force again,' Adam said flatly. 'But I'd be less than honest if I said I'll never try to make love to you. I want us to have a normal marriage, Julia. I've already told you that.'

'For how long?' Julia demanded. 'In four-year stages?'

He knew she was referring to Erica, and once again he longed to say Erica meant nothing to him. But re-membering his vow to let his actions speak for him, he did not answer the question.

'You only married me because you were a spoilt little boy who'd lost his favourite toy,' Julia went on. 'That's what women mean to you, Adam—dolls, playthings.'

'You're wrong, Julia. Wrong about a lot of things. You should stop analysing *my* reasons for marrying and start examining your own. Tell me, what made you accept me? Since it wasn't because you loved me, I assume you wanted to revenge yourself on Roy?'

'I didn't exactly throw myself into your arms,' Julia hedged. 'But I'll admit that hurt pride—my own, I mean—had something to do with it. But I think we both made a mistake, Adam, and I wish you'd realise it.'

'And do what?'

'Agree to a divorce. I'm sure Erica wouldn't object to being cited.'

The very last thing Adam wanted was a divorce, or for Erica to be involved any more in his life. Yet he could not say so without telling Julia he loved her, and once again he was forced to keep silent.

'I'm going down to breakfast,' he said brusquely, knowing she would interpret his comment as running away from the situation. 'I'll see you this evening.'

For the first time in months, Adam was glad of his full schedule that day, since it gave him little time to think of Julia. But as he left the office in the evening he could not wait to return home, and he bounded into the house feeling like a lovesick youth instead of a cynical adult.

Julia was sitting in the drawing room glancing at a magazine, and he gave her a casual smile, as if there was nothing untoward about seeing her. She looked as though she had been in the garden, for she wore a sundress and had a faintly dishevelled air which made her infinitely desirable. With an enormous effort he controlled the urge to take her upstairs and make violent love to her. One day perhaps, but right now he had to tread carefully.

'Have you remembered we're having dinner with Jack Burglass and his wife?' he asked instead.

'Of course,' Julia replied, and rose to go out.

Adam put up his hand to stop her. 'Can't we be friends, my dear?'

'Do you need a friend?'

'One always does.'

With a hard stare she walked out, and with a sigh Adam slowly went to his room to change. He was extremely depressed and wished he could cancel the dinner. Yet he knew it was better for both of them if they went out. Although he appreciated why Julia was still angry with him, he had hoped she would be more understanding by now. He had tried his best not to hurt her last night; even at the height of his passion he had been sufficiently aware to realise she was a virgin, and though it had given him a tremendous shock, it had not, unfortunately, been enough to bring him back to sanity. Nevertheless it had made him considerably more gentle with her. But if he told her this, it would only make her despise him for not being able to exercise sufficient control to leave her alone.

Still filled with self-reproach, he went down to the drawing room at seven o'clock and poured himself a stiff drink. Then he put on a record and tried to relax in an armchair. The joyful sound of Beethoven's Ninth Symphony filled the room, and gradually he was able to lose himself in the music, only returning to the present when Julia came in.

He watched her as she walked over to the cabinet, waving aside his offer to pour her a drink—and doing it for herself. In a blue silk dress the colour of her eyes, she looked sexy and provocative. It was a damn good thing they were going out. Otherwise he'd be hard put to it not to make love to her again, whether she wanted it or not. The thought scared him. What was happening to his control—his much vaunted ability to be in command of himself? Julia had made him emotionally vulnerable and he must guard against it. Standing up abruptly, he switched off the hi-fi.

'Let's go, Julia, or we'll be late.'

Setting down her half finished drink, she obeyed him without protest, almost as if she guessed his tension,

though she did not speak until they had left the house
and were walking to the car.

'Will Erica be there tonight?' she asked.

'I haven't a clue. It isn't the kind of thing I'd ask,
anyway.' Adam started up the engine.

'Doesn't Jack know you love her?'

'He might have wondered if we were having an affair,'
Adam replied as they pulled away, 'but I don't think he
ever thought we were in love.'

'Typical. Men tend not to identify love with
mistresses.'

'Some do,' said Adam. 'Love can hit you at any time,
and often most unexpectedly.'

'You can't be talking from experience,' Julia retorted
flippantly. 'You'd never let any emotion catch *you*
unawares.'

Adam's hands tightened on the wheel. If only he could
tell her how wrong she was! Yet as he lifted his foot from
the accelerator to turn to her, he was hooted from behind
and had to increase speed again. But he was glad the
opportunity had passed, for he must first convince her by
his actions: only then could he put his feelings into words.

How could I have stopped loving Erica just like that?
he asked himself for the umpteenth time. Perhaps the
answer was that he had never loved her at all. So what
had made her desirable? It couldn't have been her looks,
for he had known far lovelier women. Nor her wit, which
was cruel. If only he really stopped to think, and was
honest with himself, he must shamefacedly admit it was
her social position.

Grimly he analysed it. Kenneth Dukes had been his
first big client. With his great wealth and ancient name,
he had tended to regard most people as socially inferior,
and that included Adam. But as the years went by, Adam
had won Kenneth Dukes's respect, and they had become
firm friends. Yet there were times when Kenneth still
behaved insultingly.

As he waited for the traffic lights to change, Adam
remembered the occasion he had been invited to spend a
weekend at Kenneth's country estate in Scotland.
Kenneth had made it abundantly clear that he realised
Adam knew little about living in a large house, and
nothing whatever about hunting and shooting, and upper
class life in general. His condescending attitude had in-
furiated Adam, and it had been balm to his pride when
Kenneth's wife had made it more than plain she was attracted to him. Yet he had steered clear of any involvement with her until her marriage to Kenneth had become
a mere façade, though even then she had been the one to
make the first move.

The lights changed and Adam moved the car forward.
Seeing his affair with Erica in this new light, he recognised
a side to himself which filled him with abhorrence. Pride
had driven him into Erica's willing arms; pride had made
him ask Julia to marry him, pride had made him
eventually take her by force. God, he was despicable!

A young girl suddenly darted in front of the car and he
slammed on the brakes. Julia jerked forward and Adam's
hand shot out to steady her.

'Sorry about that,' he apologised.

'I'm wearing my safely belt,' she said coolly. 'I don't
need your help.'

Adam's lips tightened, though he did not reply until they
reached the Burglasses' house. 'Let's try to behave like a
loving couple, Julia, and not as if we're in the midst of a row.'

'You needn't worry,' she said sarcastically. 'I won't do
anything to embarrass you. *I* made a promise too, when I
married you. And *I* won't go back on my word.'

Nor did she, but acted the adoring wife so superbly
that Adam was almost fooled. His new-found love for her
made him see her with different eyes every time he looked
at her. He marvelled that he had known her for four years
without being aware of her as a woman. Yet he had
always been so sure he knew himself well, which went to

show what an ass he was. He gave a sudden short laugh, and the woman sitting next to him looked startled.

'A private joke,' he apologised, then turned to give her his full attention.

Throughout the meal he was intensely conscious of Julia opposite him; hearing every word she said, even when he was in conversation with others. Eavesdropping was something which had stood him in good stead in business, but he hadn't had much occasion to use it in his private life. Julia was talking animatedly with a man who was chairman of an insurance company in Canada, and Adam's ears pricked up when he heard Toronto mentioned. Then he heard the name Roy, and knew Julia's former fiancé had worked for the man. Jealousy seared through him and he spoke her name sharply.

Startled, she looked his way, and he gave a sheepish smile. 'Nothing, my dear. I just wanted to know if you're all right.'

'Why shouldn't I be?'

Her voice trembled and her cheeks went pink, and accusing himself for all kinds of a fool, Adam realised how easily his remark could be misconstrued. As indeed it was, if Betty Burglass's arch look was anything to go by. It was only as they left the dinner table that Julia, stopping by his side, confirmed his stupidity.

'Why did you make such a silly remark?' she whispered. 'Every woman here now thinks I'm pregnant.'

'It wouldn't be a scandal if you were. You're wearing a wedding ring, Julia.'

'Thanks for telling me. I was beginning to think it was a ball and chain!'

Adam gripped her arm, uncaring that she winced with pain. 'Next time, don't sit opposite to me and talk about your ex-fiancé,' he grated.

'How clever of you to overhear!'

'I've got several more clever tricks up my sleeve,' he warned, 'so don't try me too far.'

'Smile as you say it,' Julia said, her own lips curving upwards. 'Your friends are watching us and you're beginning to behave like a jealous husband.'

Adam dropped her arm instantly, and watched with smouldering eyes as she went to sit on the far side of the room. The next hour dragged interminably, and pleading an early morning appointment, he was finally able to leave before midnight. Julia sat silently beside him as they drove home, and he wished she did not look so calm and uncaring.

'Why do you dislike me so much?' he asked abruptly. 'And don't say it's only since last night, because I won't believe you.'

'Then perhaps it's better if I don't answer.'

'That's too easy a get-out. Be honest with me, Julia. Tell me what you feel about me.'

'I feel nothing.'

'If that were true, you wouldn't tense up whenever I'm near you. Nor would you glare at me the way you did tonight.'

'Perhaps I was thinking of our future,' she said.

'The distant or the immediate?'

Adam saw her shiver and he put out his hand. It missed her arm and touched her thigh, and she instantly drew back into her seat. 'Was I such a brute last night?' he demanded.

'Do you need me to tell you?'

'Can't you forgive me?'

'No.'

Accepting the futility of arguing, he stayed silent. If he believed that what she said was true, he would cut his losses this instant and suggest they part. But he was still convinced that given time, and his own changed attitude, Julia would eventually see him in a new light.

Neither of them spoke again, and as they drew up outside the house, Julia jumped out of the car and hurried inside, not even bothering to say goodnight. Fury gripped

Adam, wiping out all the resolutions he had made earlier. What was the use of playing for time? Of hoping Julia would learn to trust him and love him? She was so blinded by hatred of him she no longer saw him as a person—only as some kind of Satan. And there was only one way to make her see him as her husband: to act as one.

Resolutely he put the car away and strode to his room. Still keeping himself tightly under control, he prepared for bed, then firmly knocked on the door of Julia's room and walked in.

The frozen face she turned to him killed all his hopes of gaining her response, and silently he took possession of her, desperately hoping the gentleness of his touch would show her how much he cared. Tonight he thought only in terms of pleasing *her*, holding his own passion in check until, by soft mouth and skilful fingers, he had aroused her to a fever pitch of longing. She might profess to hate him, but by God, she wanted him! He was aware of it in the trembling of her limbs, the dampness of her skin, the panting gasps she gave as he plundered her mouth and took possession of her body. Yet never by a word did she say so, and when he lay exhausted beside her, she instantly moved away from him and closed her eyes, looking so much like a broken doll that he was sick with self-loathing.

'Don't look like that,' he begged. 'I can't bear it.'

'*I* have to bear it.' Her voice was ragged. 'Go away, Adam. You've used me for tonight, so go away.'

'Is that how you really feel?' he said heavily. 'As if you've been used?'

'Worse,' she said. 'I feel soiled.'

Horror gripped him. He had hoped the act of love would show Julia what he was still afraid to put into words, yet he saw how unrealistic he had been. Women were different from men in this respect. They had to feel they were loved before they could enjoy physical possession; and since Julia did not feel this, she was disgusted by his need of her. Yet he knew he wouldn't be able to keep away from her; not now he had tasted her sweetness.

'Wouldn't any woman do?' she asked into the silence. 'Why does it have to be me?'

'Because you're my wife and I love you.' The words were said and he could not retract them; wouldn't have done, even if he had been able to. 'I love you, Julia. Don't you know that?'

She laughed, a harsh, shrill laugh. 'You must really think I'm a fool if you expect me to believe you. You want me because you can't have Erica. That's all it is, Adam, so don't grace it with the name of love. My God! you don't even know the meaning of the word. I'd respect you more if you just admitted it was passion.'

'Very well then, it's passion,' he grated. 'Does that suit you better?'

'At least it's the truth—which makes it less despicable.'

With a groan he flung himself upon her, kissing her deeply, savouring her warmth and softness and losing himself in his burgeoning desire. Words of love trembled on his lips, but he forced them back, knowing he dared not utter them.

'I want you,' he said against her throat. 'At least you'll believe that, won't you? I'll never stop wanting you, Julia. So you'd better get used to the idea.'

Silence was her only reply. Silence and docile acceptance as he took possession of her body. But not of her heart, he knew, and the realisation made his conquering of her a bitter-sweet emotion.

CHAPTER TEN

JULIA, no actress at the best of times, decided she deserved a medal for the performance she gave during the weeks that followed.

After the night of the Burglasses' party she was careful to conceal all her emotions, particularly the tormenting desire that rose in her whenever Adam came near her. Yet the knowledge that his passion held no vestige of love acted as a brake upon her own love, giving her the strength to remain cold and quiescent in his arms, when all she wanted was to respond with abandon; to touch him as intimately as he touched her; to explore the secret places of his body and feel his arousal.

Yet never by word or gesture did she let him guess this, and the heat of his passion for her was flamed by the fan of his desire. That it was a strong desire was evidenced by the frequency of his demands, and every night he came to her bed, taking her silently, gently, slowly; cradling her close and sometimes muttering deep in his throat, though what he said was always unintelligible.

Sometimes he would stay the whole night, lying close beside her, and those were the times she dreaded most, for she knew an intense longing to curl up next to him and rest her head upon his shoulder; to tell him all the secrets of her innermost heart, and have him respond by telling her his own. *That* was what love was all about; not a mindless coming together like copulating animals, but an interweaving of soul and heart. Yet resolutely she kept her distance, refusing to give him the satisfaction of knowing she loved him. How triumphant he would be if she did; seeing it as a sign that his plan to conquer her by physical means had succeeded. Never, she vowed to herself

each time he left her. Never would she admit she loved a
man who was only using her to satisfy himself; who was
still besotted by another woman, yet so coldbloodedly
determined not to play second fiddle to that woman's
money that he had forced himself to turn to someone else.

Adam knew nothing of real love. Had he done, he
would have conquered his pride and remained with Erica,
uncaring of what his friends thought. Anyway, most of
them worshipped money too much to have done anything
other than applaud his decision. Even Adam's contention
that he wanted his children born in wedlock didn't ring
true, for in this day and age he could have had them
without arousing shame, and legitimised them in four
years' time when Erica would be free to become his wife.
The more Julia thought about his behaviour the more she
condemned it. Adam's pride, his obsession to come first,
had made him reject his true love and take second best.
And a man capable of doing this did not deserve to know
that, in so doing, he had uncovered another fount of love.

Yet though Julia constantly found reasons for hiding
her feelings for Adam, it was becoming increasingly difficult. His lovemaking was disclosing all the hidden passion
within her and showing her the depths of response of
which she was capable. Only the knowledge that he was
still seeing Erica acted as a brake upon her, firming her
resolve to retain her *own* pride. At least Adam had taught
her that much.

'It beats me the way Erica Dukes still runs after him,'
Susan remarked when Julia was lunching with her one
day in November.

Although Julia had not invited Susan home again—
disliking the girl's open envy too much to have her as a
close friend—she still saw her from time to time, feeling
the need to talk with someone from her own background,
whose ethos was work instead of the social butterflies she
generally met through Adam. Not that she herself was
any better at the moment, for she too was living a life of

idleness. But not for long, she vowed. One day soon she would find a job and become a person in her own right.

'Only yesterday,' Susan went on, 'she barged into the office at five-thirty. She knows your husband's usually free at that time, and she just hung around waiting to see him.'

'I'm sure he did,' Julia said casually. 'After all, she's an important client. Kenneth Dukes had interests all over the world.'

'And the lovely Erica's trying to persuade Mr Lester to fly around with her to check up on them. I suppose you know that?'

'Of course,' Julia lied.

'Is he going?' Susan asked, then said hurriedly: 'Don't answer if you don't want to. I keep forgetting you're my boss's wife and no longer his secretary.'

'I do wish you'd call him Adam,' Julia said in pretended exasperation, glad of something on which to vent her anger—however unimportant.

'I call him Mr Lester in the office,' Susan replied, 'so it's become a habit.'

'Sorry,' Julia said contritely. 'I understand.'

'You're too understanding,' her friend declared. 'That's your trouble. If Adam was *my* husband, I'd scratch Erica Dukes' eyes out. Anyway, even if you're so sure of him, I still think you should pretend to be jealous. It's good for a man's ego.'

'Adam and I don't need to pretend with each other. We're close enough to behave naturally.' Julia almost laughed as she gave utterance to the lie. The closeness of their physical union had only widened the gulf between them, making her hate him for his power over her.

'You *are* happy, aren't you, Julia?' Susan asked unexpectedly. 'I get the impression something's worrying you.'

'There's nothing wrong with me whatever,' Julia said evenly. 'I'm a bit tired, that's all.'

'Too many disturbed nights?' Susan asked mischievously.

'Keep your imagination for the office!'

The two girls looked at each other and chuckled, and Julia was delighted to have passed off the awkward moment so casually. But when she returned home and looked at herself in the hall mirror, she knew Susan's comment was justified. She was pale and there was a tension in her expression which should not have been there. Still, it wasn't surprising, for on the physical side alone she was exhausted. Adam came to her room nearly every night, making love to her over and over again, as if tormented by spirits that would give him no rest. Even on the rare nights he stayed away, she lay trembling, part of her not wanting him, the other desperately aching for his touch.

What's to become of me? she wondered desperately. Where will it all end? Sighing heavily, she went into the drawing room, stopping involuntarily as she saw the recipient of her thoughts in an armchair.

'You're home early,' she commented, her cool voice giving no sign of the anguish inside her.

'I have to go to Rome,' Adam told her. 'Hank Renson, of Chicago Steel, is having trouble with his subsidiary in Italy, and I said I'd meet him out there.'

'How long will you be away?'

'Two or three days. I'll call and tell you when I'll be back.'

'Why bother?' Julia shrugged. 'I'm always here.'

'Good,' Adam said without expression.

Hating him for his arrogance, Julia walked through to the terrace. The garden was an oasis of quiet and one could hardly credit that barely twenty yards away the traffic was roaring down the road. Had it not been for the houses on either side, one could almost have felt in the country. Julia suddenly recollected that she hadn't done anything about finding them a country house. It was surprising Adam hadn't made some sarcastic comment about it. She would see some estate agents while he was away. It would give her something to do and stop her brooding.

'You're looking very lovely, Julia.' Adam had come up behind her.

'Susan thought I looked pale,' she replied, keeping her head averted.

It was the wrong thing to say, for Adam stretched out a hand and turned her to face him. Frowning, he stared at her.

'You don't look pale to me. In fact you're flushed.' His voice deepened. 'But then I always have that effect on you. You're still not used to me, are you, Julia? But you will be, I promise you that.'

'You make it sound like a threat!'

'*You* make it a threat,' he said heavily. 'If you——'

A sound behind them made him stop, and he looked over his shoulder to see the chauffeur.

'I'll be right with you,' he called to the man, then bent and kissed Julia's cheek. 'I'm sorry I have to rush away like this. I wanted to talk to you.'

'You've nothing to say that I want to hear,' she replied stonily. 'I wish you'd realise that.'

'Still hating me?' he asked.

'More than ever.'

Silently he left her, and the moment she was alone Julia wished she had controlled her temper. Yet his closeness aroused her so much she did indeed hate him.

The telephone rang and she heard Emilio answer it. It must have been for Adam, because he did not come in search of her, and later, as she was on her way upstairs and saw him in the hall, she asked who had called.

'Mrs Dukes,' he replied. 'She rang to ask if Mr Lester had already left for the airport. She said there was no message as she would be seeing him in Rome.'

Julia was glad she had the presence of mind to continue walking up the stairs. But how she got to the top without falling, she did not know, for she was shaking with humiliation. How dared Adam lie to her like this? Or did he think she wouldn't find out? She banged the bedroom door behind her and tore off her jacket, convinced Erica had telephoned here deliberately.

Wave after wave of jealousy swept over her, and blindly she reached for the telephone and dialled Roy's number. A pity she had no other man to call, for it seemed unfair to use Roy like this. Still, she shouldn't have any qualms; he hadn't played fair with her in the past.

'Roy?' she said as soon as he came on the line. 'You said I could ring you when I was free to see you. I hope you meant it?'

'Try me,' he replied eagerly.

'How about tonight?'

'Wonderful. I'll collect you at eight,' he said without hesitation. 'Is there anywhere special you'd like to go?'

'Some place where we can dance,' she said. This would lessen the need for conversation.

'I'm not very well up on those kind of places,' Roy confessed.

'Then *I'll* book for us.'

Determined to enjoy herself, Julia put on one of her most daring dresses, and when Roy came into the drawing room, prompt as ever, he could not disguise his admiration.

'Much as I hate to admit it, Julia, marriage agrees with you,' he told her. 'I've never seen you look more beautiful.'

'And I've never known you so full of compliments,' she smiled. 'I'm glad you were free at such short notice.'

'Where's your husband?'

'He had to go to Rome for a few days.' Julia longed to add: 'with another woman' but restrained herself, knowing that to say such a thing would only increase her humiliation. 'Let's go,' she said, turning to the door, and then stopped. 'Oh dear, I haven't offered you a drink. What will you have?'

'Let's wait till we get to the restaurant,' he replied. 'It's bad enough taking out another man's wife without also drinking his whisky!'

Julia looked at Roy's serious face: the eyes watchful, the mouth small and slightly turned down at the corners; the carefully brushed hair and conservative dark suit. Was it possible she had ever considered marrying such a sobersides?

'Adam would be delighted to know you're taking me out,' she answered him. 'He doesn't like me sitting at home twiddling my thumbs, so you needn't feel guilty at having a drink here.'

'Next time,' Roy answered, leading her out.

She paused in the hall to slip on a wisp of beaded silk to cover her shoulders, and he looked at it with slight concern.

'Will you be warm enough in that, Julia?'

'We're going in the car, aren't we? Anyway, don't you know the old proverb: To be fashionable, one must suffer a little?'

'No,' he smiled. 'Nor do I agree with it. I'd prefer to be less fashionable—and less likely to catch pneumonia!'

She laughed. 'Well, at least aim for a happy medium.'

'Meaning?'

'That you still dress too conservatively.'

'I can't see myself in tight-fitting jeans or suede suits.'

'Not quite *that*,' she agreed. 'But at least throw away the pinstripes and clerical greys.'

'I'm too old to change my image,' Roy stated. 'You can't turn me into a jet-setter like your husband.'

'Adam isn't in the least like a jet-setter,' she protested. 'He may jet round the world, but it's purely for business.' Resolutely she pushed away thoughts of Erica in Rome with him. 'Come on, we'd better go or we'll be late.'

Julia had booked a table at a restaurant in Berkeley Square. It was very much in fashion at the moment, and she and Adam had been there several times with his friends. Funny that she still didn't regard any of them as her own friends. Maybe it was because she didn't regard herself as genuinely his wife. It was a ludicrous admission, bearing in mind his constant lovemaking, but—no, she corrected herself, love had nothing to do with it: that was the trouble.

'What an unusual room.'

Roy's comment brought Julia back to the present, and she looked at the trellis-lined walls—all intertwined with flowers—the thickly carpeted floor, grass green, naturally, and the candlelit tables that bordered the small dance floor. The clientele were as elegant as the decor, and Roy noticed it and looked vaguely ill at ease as they were warmly greeted by the head waiter and shown to an excellent table.

'You must come here quite often,' he said.

'I do. It's one of Adam's favourite places.'

'I'm glad you've done so well for yourself,' Roy added, and reddened furiously as he saw the look Julia gave him. 'I mean it,' he apologised, 'I wasn't being snide. You've married well and I'm glad. Even though I'd give my right arm to be in Adam Lester's place.'

'You were,' she reminded him before she could stop herself.

'I know. That's what makes it so distressing for me.'

'Stop thinking about the past and concentrate on the present,' Julia advised. 'Being upset won't do your digestion any good.'

Roy smiled reluctantly, but as the meal progressed and the wine bottle was slowly emptied, he became far better company. Though basically dull, he was interesting when he spoke of his work; and his months in Canada had undoubtedly widened his horizons, so that the hours passed far more swiftly than Julia would have supposed. It was only as they were coming off the dance floor later in the evening that he allowed himself to become personal, obviously too moved by her closeness to monitor his feelings.

'I still love you, Julia,' he said jerkily. 'If anything went wrong with your marriage ... I know I shouldn't be saying this, and that I'll regret it tomorrow, but——'

'I'd never marry you, Roy,' Julia cut across him, 'not even if I were free. I'm not saying it to be spiteful, but because I don't want you wasting your life regretting the might-have-beens.'

As if her words acted as a spur, Roy made a visible effort to overcome his emotion, and was soon regaling her with amusing anecdotes about his short stay in Toronto.

Julia tried to show an interest in what he was saying, but found herself listening with only half an ear, her mind in Rome with Adam and Erica. Were they sharing a bedroom or did they maintain the proprieties and have two? Jealousy was like gall inside her, making her thoughts so bitter she felt physically ill. She must have lost colour, for Roy stopped in mid-sentence and regarded her with such concern that she made a great effort to smile.

'It's rather hot in here,' she murmured. 'I'll have another coffee. It should make me feel better.'

'Fresh air will make you better still,' Roy retorted, and called instantly for the bill.

Gratefully Julia went outside with him, and he made her stroll slowly around the square before going to their car. Only when he had satisfied himself that her colour was back to normal did he drive her home. His solicitude was touching and made her regret going out with him and arousing his hopes that they might have a future together.

'Will you let me see you again before your husband returns?' he asked as they stopped outside her front door.

'I don't think it's fair to you if I say yes. It was naughty of me to call you this afternoon.'

'Rubbish. I love you, Julia, and not seeing you won't alter the way I feel.'

'It will, if you go out with other girls.'

'I'll go out with other girls when I can't see *you*. Please, my dear, I'm not a child. I know exactly what I'm doing, and if you're free to go out with other men, then——'

'Not with other men,' Julia said quickly, anxious not to give him the wrong impression. 'Only with *you*. I'm not looking for an affair, Roy. I thought I'd already made that clear?'

'As crystal,' he answered. 'So stop worrying and tell me what time to call for you tomorrow, and where you fancy going.'

The next night Roy took her to a concert at the Festival Hall, and on the third evening Julia invited him over to dinner.

'Are you sure it's all right for me to come here?' he asked anxiously, as she met him at the door. 'I almost called you this afternoon to suggest we went out instead.'

'Whatever for? We're not doing anything wrong. You're an old friend and it's quite the fashion to see old flames—even Adam makes a habit of it.'

'I can imagine him having had quite a conflagration in his time,' Roy said wryly. 'I remember the things you used to tell me about him. I still can't get over you marrying him.'

'Well, I did. And I've got you to thank for all this.' She waved her hand round the sumptuously furnished room. 'See what a good turn you did me?'

'And myself a bad one,' he muttered. 'Oh, Julia, if only——'

'Don't say it, Roy. If you do, I'll stop seeing you.'

As she said it, she knew there shouldn't be any 'if' about it. To let Roy remain in her life was storing up hurt for him, and she had to discontinue their relationship. If she were as tough as Erica, she wouldn't mind using another person as a sop to her pride. But she wasn't, and she couldn't pretend.

They were sitting in the drawing room having coffee

when Julia heard footsteps in the hall. She had not heard a car draw up but immediately guessed it was Adam. Her cup shook in her hand as he entered the room, and she set it quickly down in front of her. His eyes took in the tableau before him, and not a muscle in his face moved as he looked at Julia and the man beside her. Showing unexpected self-possession, Roy rose and introduced himself.

'If you'd let me know you were returning so early,' Julia said, 'we'd have waited dinner.'

'I wanted to surprise you,' Adam replied. 'And I see I have.'

'A very pleasant surprise, darling,' Julia said sweetly. 'Would you like me to get you a snack?'

'No, thanks, I've already eaten.'

'With Erica?' she asked blandly.

His eyes narrowed. 'No. She's still in Rome. She had some business to finalise.'

'Other business?'

Adam gave Julia a hard look before going over to pour himself a brandy. He came and sat beside her on the settee and idly caught hold of her hand as he chatted to Roy. With the charm she always associated with him he swiftly put the other man at ease, and they were soon gossiping about mutual people they knew in the City, for all the world as if *they* were the two friends and Julia the odd one out.

It was eleven before Roy finally rose to leave, and Julia went with him to the door.

'I can see why you married Adam Lester,' he said softly. 'And also why you told me we've no future together. You make a striking-looking pair, my dear. I could never compete with him. He's way out of my league.'

Julia said nothing, and the next moment Roy was gone. She was glad he had finally conceded defeat and hoped he'd soon find someone else. Regardless of how he felt about her, she knew they were incompatible. Sighing, she forced herself to return to the drawing room, knowing

that if she didn't, Adam would think she had something
to hide.

'I hope I didn't spoil your cosy little evening?' he
greeted her as she rejoined him.

'Not at all. I can always see Roy another time—when
you're otherwise engaged.'

'If you're subtly referring to my being in Rome with
Erica,' Adam said, 'I give you my word I didn't invite
her.'

'You mean it was pure coincidence?'

'No, it was damned bloody-mindedness! She was in my
office when Hank Renson telephoned, and she heard him
arranging to meet him in Rome.'

Julia could well believe it of Erica, but was reluctant to
admit it.

'You could have refused to see her,' she said instead.

'I only saw her once during the three days,' he replied.
'And that was because she forced herself on me.' He hesitated. 'Well, it would be truer to say Hank rather fancied
her, and she played along with him.'

'Is he rich?' Julia asked sarcastically.

'Extremely. But unfortunately Erica only wants forbidden fruit.'

'You're only forbidden for another three and a half
years,' Julia retorted.

'Still playing the same tune?' Adam asked sourly. 'Since
you refuse to believe anything I say about Erica, it's
pointless discussing her. However, before you continue
your role of aggrieved wife, I should remind you that
people in glasshouses shouldn't throw bricks. Or do you
expect me to believe your ex-fiancé came here un-
invited?'

'Not at all,' Julia stated. 'I asked him.'

'Before or after you found out that Erica was in
Rome?'

'Before,' Julia lied.

'I see.' Adam banged his glass down on the table and

went to the door. 'I'll say goodnight here, Julia. I'm tired.'

Julia remained downstairs for a long while before going to her room. Had Adam used tiredness merely as an excuse for not coming to her tonight, or had a hectic three nights with Erica jaded his sexual appetite? If only she knew the truth!

Jumping to her feet, she paced the room in a frenzy of torment. Love, jealousy, anger, hurt, all melded into one aching pain that racked her body and left her too exhausted to fight any longer; too exhausted to pretend. It was a good thing Adam wouldn't be with her tonight, or she would have lost complete control and would either have given herself to him with total abandon, or screamed at him never to touch her again unless he wanted her to walk out and leave him, regardless of the bargain they had made. But no such choice was necessary. Adam would keep his distance because he was too clever to chance his luck.

For the next few weeks he was exceptionally busy, leaving the house before nine and rarely returning before eight when, after a hasty meal, he retired to his study with a bulging briefcase. Once, Julia went in to him at midnight to ask if he wanted a hot drink, and he had to focus on her for several seconds before realising she was there. Then he shook his head abruptly, as if unable to bear a moment's interruption. Next day Julia instructed Emilio to leave a thermos and some sandwiches in the study each night, sure that if they were there, Adam would nibble at them.

Her love for him made her keenly observant of him, and she noticed he had lost weight since his trip to Rome. Was it because of the dilemma in which he found himself—wanting Erica and seeing no immediate escape from Julia? Having made their marriage a real one, he now had to wait the statutory three years before obtaining a divorce. Yet he never spoke to her of wanting his freedom;

in fact he barely spoke to her at all. He was polite enough when they met, but the friendly, early days of their marriage had long since gone.

The cessation of his lovemaking came as a relief, though Julia wondered if he was waiting for her to make the next move. If so he would have a long wait. Right now she wasn't sure whether to stay with him and hope he would come to his senses over Erica, or leave and make a new life for herself. But what life could she have without Adam? The answer was too depressing to contemplate, even though she knew they could not continue like this. But only Adam had the power to resolve the situation: either Erica in three years' time or Julia now? It seemed he had not yet decided, and until he did she had to find the strength to accept the situation.

Ten days after Adam's return from Rome, Julia asked Roy to take her to dinner. At least it was better than sitting alone moping.

'I was surprised to hear from you,' Roy confessed when they were facing each other across the table in the White Tower, one of the best of the Greek restaurants in Soho.

'Well, Adam's working himself into the ground and I'm bored out of my skull.'

'Bored women are dangerous women.'

'That's a very profound statement,' she teased.

'I'm not joking. Your husband's a fool if he doesn't realise it.'

'He's too sure of me,' Julia lied.

'Yet you don't look happy.' Roy eyed her speculatively. '*Something's* worrying you, my dear, and I'd like to help you. A trouble shared is a trouble halved, you know.'

'I haven't any troubles for us to share,' Julia asserted. 'I can't imagine why you think I should have.'

'Because I know a little bit about your character, and you aren't acting true to form. If there was nothing wrong with your marriage, you wouldn't be having dinner with me. And don't give me the excuse that you were bored or lonely.'

'Okay then, I won't. But let's just say I don't want to talk about Adam and myself.'

'Fair enough. As long as you remember that if you're ever in need of a father confessor, you can count on me.'

As she entered the house in Chester Street later that night, Julia decided she liked Roy more now than at any time since she had known him. If they had met after her marriage to Adam there might have been a chance of their becoming good friends. But unfortunately the past would always be between them, and Adam was a stumbling block too. He was far too possessive to accept her ex-fiancé as one of their friends.

She was crossing the hall when Adam came out of his study. He looked tired and dishevelled, and his shirt sleeves were pushed up above his elbows.

'You're back early,' he said tonelessly.

'It's midnight.'

'That late? I didn't realise.'

'You never do when you work.' Julia glanced over his shoulder at the jumble of papers on his desk. 'I suppose all this burning of the midnight oil is absolutely necessary?'

'You don't think I'm doing it for the fun of it, do you? Or perhaps you think I'm trying to ease my aching heart?'

'If your heart aches you've only yourself to blame. If you want to live with Erica, and end our arrangement, just tell me.'

'Would you go?'

'Of course.'

Adam's face hardened. 'I've no intention of asking you to leave.'

'Even though you're unhappy?'

'You mean even though *you* are. If you weren't married to me, would you go back with Roy?'

Bitter that he could even ask, Julia forced herself to look at him impassively. 'Believe what you like, Adam.

But if you *do* think that, why do you insist we stay together?'

'Because you're my wife. And even in today's emancipated society, marriage still means something.'

'Not our marriage,' she flared. 'Neither of us married for love, and I'd feel nothing about ending it.'

'We won't end it,' he said harshly.

'You'll change your mind once Erica's free to marry you.'

'Don't tell me you're pleading her cause?' Adam asked derisively. 'Or are you really pleading your own? But it won't do any good. You'll have to make it clear to Roy that I'm holding you to the bargain we made.'

'No one must ever touch anything that belongs to you, must they, Adam?'

Julia pushed past him and went to her room, slamming the door behind her. Nervously she wondered if he would follow her to continue the argument, but then she heard the door of his study close. She gave a sigh. How long could they live together like this? One of them had to bend to the will of the other, and she was determined it wouldn't be her.

Bending to the dressing table to take off her earrings, she caught sight of her face. How pale she looked; nothing like a wife of six months. No wonder Roy had said she was unhappy! But short of breaking her word to Adam and walking out, she did not know how to solve the situation. At least if she left, she would stand *some* chance of rebuilding her life; remaining here, she had no chance whatever.

'Pack and go,' she muttered to her reflection. 'Maybe if you don't see him, you'll forget him.'

Yet even as she said it she knew how untrue it was. Living with Adam or not, he would always be entrenched in her heart. And since he was, she might as well remain here. At least she would have the satisfaction of seeing him every day.

Soberly she undressed and climbed into bed, picturing Adam working at his desk. Poor Adam; too busy regretting his lost love to see the love so close to him. Tears flowed down her cheeks and she began to cry: for herself, for Adam, and for all the might-have-beens.

CHAPTER ELEVEN

Two days later, Adam again had to go to Rome, but this time he stressed the fact that Erica would not be there.

'It doesn't matter to me if she is,' said Julia.

'You're very understanding,' he retorted.

'I'm sorry I can't return the compliment.'

'So you should be. After all, I haven't forbidden you to see your ex-fiancé.'

'Not in so many words. But you showed your disapproval quite clearly when I invited him here.'

Before Adam could reply, the chauffeur came into the hall to collect his case. Only then did Julia notice he seemed to be taking an unusually large one for such a short trip.

'I may have to fly on to Johannesburg,' he said, seeing her eyes on his case. 'I'll let you know.'

He went out to the car and Julia followed him, standing on the steps as he took the seat beside the chauffeur. It was all she could do to stop herself from running after him and begging him to take her along. But instead she remained where she was: coolly smiling, and giving no sign of the emotions raging inside her.

'Take care of yourself while I'm away,' Adam called through the open window, and wished he dared tell her what an exquisite picture she made in her green dress, with her lustrous auburn hair cascading around her shoulders. How Titian would have loved to paint her!

The car moved off and Julia waved her arm at him: the loving wife speeding her husband on his way. Well, that only went to show how easily pictures could lie. He settled back and forced himself to think of the hectic few days ahead of him. He hoped he wouldn't have to fly to

South Africa. Each moment away from Julia was a moment lost; a moment that had to be made up again. How much longer could he go on hiding his love for her? He had hoped their physical closeness would help her to see him as a warm-blooded man and not simply a business machine, but it appeared to have done the reverse. She was colder than ever towards him, and he was beginning to realise that winning her affection might take him much longer than he had anticipated. The return of her ex-fiancé hadn't been a help either. Even if Julia had been getting over her love for Roy, having him re-enter her life was undoubtedly keeping her feelings for him alive.

Adam bit back a sigh. What a mess things were! He hadn't been able to touch Julia for weeks. Not because he had ceased wanted her but because his need was so great he had been scared of losing control and forcing her into total submission; of *making* her respond to him, making her hold him intimately and kiss him with abandon. But even had he succeeded in breaking through her icy reserve, it would have achieved nothing except to increase her disgust with him. For this reason he had stayed away from her. But he knew he couldn't carry on like this. The situation had to be resolved one way or the other. As soon as he returned home he would tell Julia the truth; admit that his love for Erica was dead—that it had only been infatuation and that he was now capable of so much more. And all because of Julia herself, who had shown him that poverty was much more than a lack of money. It was also a lack of trust in another human being; a lack of confidence in oneself. This last had been the hardest lesson of all for him to learn. Never had he believed that he—so successful a lawyer that tycoons all over the world sought his advice—should still lack personal confidence in himself.

But once he had started examining Julia's statement he had gradually come to acknowledge that she was right. It hadn't been easy, and for months he had denied it, but his growing love for her had done what a psychologist might have taken months to achieve, and as he gradually accepted the truth of what she said, everything else had fallen easily into place. He pulled a face. Never easily. Only if Julia loved him would life be easy; until she did, it was pure unadulterated hell.

'We're nearly there, sir,' his chauffeur said. 'We made extra good time today.'

'So I see.' With an effort Adam returned to the present, knowing he must marshall all his acumen for the hectic few days ahead of him.

Julia waited on the steps until Adam's car disappeared round a bend in the road. Only then did she re-enter the house. How empty it was without him! Even though he had been immersed in work and she had hardly seen him in the past weeks, just knowing he was there had made her feel good. But now the rooms were desolate and silent, and the indifference which she had assumed for Adam's benefit gave way to depression. Disconsolately she wandered through the drawing room into the garden. Now would be as good a time as any to continue the search for a country house, she thought. Yet it seemed a wasted effort. She could not see a continuing future with Adam and had no inclination to find him a home which he would eventually share with another woman—probably Erica. Angrily she wondered why she was still waiting for him to end their marriage, when it was so easy for her to end it herself by packing up and walking out. The luxury of being his wife meant nothing to her, and though she had to admit she enjoyed having money to spend and servants to wait on her, she wouldn't find it a hardship to return to her old way of life. So what was stopping her? Masochism? No, it was more than that. It was the fact that she had made a promise to remain Adam's wife for as long as he needed her, and she could not lightly break her word.

Sinking on to a garden seat, she lifted her face to the

sun and tried to let its warmth relax her. Slowly the tension left her body and, as it did, she became aware that she was hungry. Jumping up, she walked round the house into the kitchen. The housekeeper was making aspic and had reached the laborious stage of beating the egg whites into the stock. Waving her to carry on, Julia helped herself to some home-made wholemeal bread, liberally buttering two slices and covering them thickly with strawberry jam—also home-made.

'I wish you always eat like this,' Maria grunted. 'You and the *signore* have lost a lot of weight.'

'It isn't because we don't like your cooking,' Julia assured her. 'On the contrary, we both love it. But we haven't done it justice lately because—because . . .'

'Because love robs you of appetite,' Maria beamed. 'I understand all that. But you are still much too thin, *signora*.'

'Well, I'm making up for it with the five hundred calories I've just had. If I go on like this, I'll soon put it all on again.'

'Eat something more,' Maria pleaded. 'I make you an omelette, yes?'

'No,' Julia smiled. 'I'm much too full.'

Yet as she returned to the garden and sat down beneath the apple tree, she again felt an odd sinking in the pit of her stomach, as if she had not eaten for days. Maybe it was because she wasn't eating regularly. She had better make sure she did. The last thing she wanted was to be ill and become a burden on Adam.

With few friends to whom she could turn, Julia invited Susan to dinner and to stay the night. The girl had now started taking Julia's changed circumstances for granted, and no longer made envious comments about it, so that their relationship had, over the past months, become more natural.

Susan was more than delighted to accept the invitation, and came direct to the house from the office, accepting

Julia's offer of the loan of a nightdress.

'I feel as though I'm coming to a five-star hotel,' she grinned, entering the beautifully furnished bedroom and dancing around the satin-covered bed. 'The only thing that'll spoil it is having to get up at seven-thirty to get ready for the rush hour.'

'Then next time you'll have to come for the weekend,' Julia grinned. 'Providing you promise not to call my husband "Mr Lester".'

Susan grinned back, though the humour left her face as she eyed Julia's slender body. 'You're getting terribly thin, you know. Are you sure you aren't ill?'

'Of course I'm sure. But I may be a bit anaemic, which is probably why I'm looking run-down. I'll pop in and see the doctor tomorrow.'

'Why didn't you go away with Adam?'

'He didn't ask me,' Julia said truthfully. 'He knew he'd be very tied up, and he didn't want any distractions.'

'And you certainly would be,' Susan agreed. 'I've never seen you more beautiful. It suits you to be emaciated, old dear. It accentuates your cheekbones and gives you interesting hollows.'

Julia studied her reflection intently that night, and though she knew Susan spoke the truth, she was far from pleased. Who wanted to look more beautiful simply because they felt ill? And she did feel ill: there was no longer any point denying it. Well, maybe 'ill' was too strong a word, but definitely off colour and lacking energy. Though her earlier promise to see a doctor had been made halfheartedly, she decided to do so first thing next day.

The moment Susan left for the office Julia rang for an appointment with her doctor. He was Adam's medical adviser too, and she had started going to him prior to her wedding, when she had needed various shots before her trip to India.

'You'd better have some preliminary tests before you come to see me,' he advised. 'Go to the Devonshire Clinic.

I'll let them know what I want them to do.'

'Can't I go to a hospital?' Julia asked, unwilling to run up a large bill at a private clinic.

'No,' came the peremptory answer. 'Adam wouldn't like it. If you go to a hospital, you'll have to wait weeks for your results. You women astonish me. You think nothing of spending a hundred pounds on a dress; but you quibble at paying anything for your health.'

Appreciating the comment, Julia agreed to do as Dr Forrester said, and spent almost the entire afternoon undergoing tests. Probably unnecessary, she thought, but better safe than sorry.

That evening she decided to have an early night. She had television in her room and she lay back against the pillows and tried to interest herself in the goings on of a particularly stupid heroine. Her eyes were just beginning to close when the telephone rang. It was Adam calling from Rome.

'I wasn't sure if I'd find you at home,' he said, his voice so clear on the line that he could have been in the room. 'Is anyone with you?'

'Jeremy Breen,' she retorted, 'but unfortunately only his television image! I'm in bed—alone.'

'You didn't need to add the last word.' Adam's voice was clipped. 'I've never doubted your virtue.'

'And what are *you* doing?' she asked.

'I'm not in bed, neither am I alone. In fact I'm in the middle of a meeting. And with the Italians, it's a bit like being in the monkey house!'

Julia couldn't help laughing. 'I'm sure you'll be able to quieten them down. Tell me, are you going on to Johannesburg, as you thought you might?'

'Luckily, no. I've been able to settle the matter from here. So I'll be back tomorrow in time for dinner—I hope. Julia . . .'

She waited for him to finish the sentence.

'What is it?' she asked, as the silence continued.

'I—I—Damn it, I can't discuss it now. I'll wait until I see you. I have something to say—to explain. Sleep well, Julia.'

'You too.'

Slowly she replaced the receiver, wondering what it was Adam wanted to say that he couldn't tell her over the telephone. Something intimate and serious, no doubt. And that meant it concerned Erica. The thought was enough to give her a restless night, and she awoke at dawn, and was dressed and breakfasted before eight. Adam's last words kept resounding in her head and she tried to remember his exact tone. There had been a faint tremor in his voice, as if he was unsure of himself, and she wondered if he had finally come to the realisation that they could not continue their life together in this way. But what route did he want to take? Julia determined not to hazard a guess, knowing this could lead to disappointment and heartbreak. She must wait to hear the truth from Adam himself.

Promptly at eleven, she set off for her appointment with Dr Forester. His consulting rooms were in Mayfair, some twenty minutes' walk from the house, but the day was pleasant and made walking a pleasure—except for the traffic, which was more congested than ever, and sent fumes of oil and petrol into the air.

Briskly she made her way through the park to Park Lane, and reached Upper Brook Street with a few minutes to spare. Slowing her pace, she strolled down the turning. A young man in jeans eyed her with interest and then gave her an appreciative grin, which suddenly made her feel angry with herself for being so despondent. Whether Adam wanted her or not, her life was by no means over. She was only twenty-four years old, good-looking and not unintelligent. The world could still be her oyster if she had the courage to face up to the challenge of starting afresh. Let Adam do what the hell he liked!

Dr Forester's words—some few moments later—dramatically changed the pattern of Julia's thoughts, and when she eventually left his consulting room, she hardly dared believe what she had heard.

She was expecting a baby. Adam's child. The nights she had lain dormant in his arms, determined to remain unresponsive to his caresses, had nonetheless resulted in an act of creation, the seed of which she bore within her. It was, at one and the same time, a wonderful yet terrifying thought. Wonderful because it was the child of Adam, the man she loved with all her heart, and terrifying because of the knowledge that he might, even at this very moment, be making plans to end their marriage.

'Julia!' With a start, she turned and saw Erica in front of her, her blonde hair bright as a new penny in the sunlight.

'Hello, Erica,' she said quietly, 'I didn't see you.'

'Deliberately or unintentionally?'

'Why should it be deliberate?'

'Surely I don't need to answer that? You don't like me, and you make very little effort to hide it. Not that I blame you,' Erica added graciously. 'After all, you know you have the man I want, and that I intend getting him back.'

'You mean I have the man you decided you *didn't* want,' Julia said evenly, and looked over Erica's shoulder, hoping to see a taxi—anything, as a means of escape.

Erica gave a tight smile. 'I admit I behaved stupidly, and given another chance I wouldn't do it again. But unfortunately you stepped in before I realised my mistake, and——'

'I *didn't* step in,' Julia interrupted, determined to put the matter straight. 'Adam *asked* me—begged me—to marry him.'

'And you jumped at the opportunity,' Erica retorted, 'before he even had a chance to realise that *my* solution was the best.'

'For you, maybe,' Julia replied, 'but not for Adam. He

needs a home and a secure marriage.'

'You talk as if he's helpless.' Erica's brown eyes were hard as pebbles. 'He's racketed around too much for me to believe he was hankering after hearth and home. His pride was hurt because I refused to take his name until it suited me. It was nothing more than that.'

'Are you saying it suits you now?' Julia demanded.

Erica's delicate features hardened, making her look much older. 'Why don't you ask Adam, or are you scared of bringing up my name?'

'I believe in facing facts,' Julia replied, 'no matter how ugly.'

An empty taxi cruised past and she ran towards it, hand upraised. Wrenching open the door, she climbed in and gave her address, staring fixedly ahead as they pulled away from the kerb. They were halfway home when the thought of returning to the empty house and spending the afternoon alone with her chaotic thoughts was more than she could bear; and she asked the driver to take her to Oxford Street. It would do her good to be among people; to see others going about their daily lives might help her to accept that her own was but a microcosm on this planet; her unhappiness of supreme unimportance in the general scheme of things. But how difficult it was when her heart was crying out in despair. Was there any truth in Erica's insinuations? But she already knew the answer—had known it even before seeing Erica today. She was only waiting for Adam to confirm it.

'This part of Oxford Street okay?' the taxi driver asked, and Julia saw they had stopped outside Selfridge's.

She nodded and paid him off, then went into the store. It was crowded and hot, and she soon tired of being jostled and went into the street again. Slowly she ambled down South Molton Street, looking in the shop windows and trying to summon up an interest in the beautiful dresses, shoes and bags that were on display. But nothing tempted her. Soon she found herself in Grosvenor Square and saw the American Embassy with its golden eagle outlined against the sky. She had once toyed seriously with the idea of working in the States, and she wished with all her heart that she had done something about it. If she had, she wouldn't be in this present miserable predicament. She stopped walking. She was pregnant. She still couldn't accept the fact. And what on earth was she going to do with a baby?

She reached a zebra crossing and was halfway over it when she again heard her name called. Reaching the island in the centre of the road, she stopped and turned round. Roy was waving to her from the opposite pavement and she went quickly towards him.

'You're the second person I'm bumped into today,' she said.

'Who was the first?'

'Erica Dukes.'

'Your husband's ex-lady-friend?' Roy looked amused. 'I bet *her* nose was put out of joint when he married you.'

Julia nodded, not trusting herself to speak, and Roy seemed to think the subject was at an end.

'How about having lunch with me?' he suggested.

'Are you sure you have time?'

He nodded. 'Just let me make a call and then I'll be free till early afternoon.'

A quarter of an hour later they were seated at a table in the Connaught Grill, their order given, and Roy regarding her intently.

'I was going to call you some time this week,' he said. 'I wanted to let you know I'm being sent to Paris for six months.'

'Paris?' Julia was surprised. 'Are you pleased about it?'

'From a career point of view, yes. It means another rung up the ladder.'

He went on talking and Julia listened with only half an ear, her thoughts busy with her own problem. How and when was she going to tell Adam her news? As soon as he saw him tonight, or should she lead up to it gradually? A young wife would normally be bursting with excitement to tell her husband she was expecting a baby, but it was different for herself. All she felt was anxiety and despair. And heaven knew what Adam would feel. She glanced at Roy from beneath her lashes, wondering what *he* would say if she told him she was pregnant.

'I'll contact you as soon as I get back to London,' Roy said, breaking into her thoughts. 'Unless you ever find yourself in Paris, that is.'

'I doubt it,' Julia replied, amused by the thought of herself, with swollen belly, strolling down the Champs-Elysées.

'If you need me at any time,' he went on, 'don't hesitate to let me know.'

'I will,' she lied, knowing that Roy, for all his willingness, could never again be a part of her future.

It was an utterable relief when she finally found herself outside the front door of her home, and she stood there for a moment, knowing that here, in this house, had come the realisation of her love for the man she had married. It was here Adam's child had been conceived, yet she had no idea if it was here that he or she would grow up. Only one thing was certain. She must now do what was best for her baby. Her own pride was no longer important.

Adam had said he wanted to make their marriage work. For that reason he had forced her to consummate it. But the anger which had prevented her telling him she loved him had miraculously died the instant she had learned of the life she was carrying inside her. She would tell Adam she loved him regardless of how spineless it made her seem. All that mattered was for her to have the strength to build a future with him and the baby; to make his home such a warm and happy one that he would gradually find it adequate compensation. Happy to have made her decision, she went into the house.

The door leading to the drawing room was ajar and

instantly she sensed someone was there. She walked in and stopped, startled to see Adam standing by the window.

'I didn't expect you so early,' she said. 'I've been lunching with Roy.'

'Would you have put off your date if you'd known I was coming back early?'

'I'd have had nothing to put off,' she replied. 'I didn't arrange to see Roy. I bumped into him in Grosvenor Square.'

Adam's shrug made it obvious he did not believe her, and she bit her lip. The sunlight pouring in haloed his head and outlined his shoulders, making him look taller and broader. But thinner too, she thought with a pang, noticing how pale he was beneath his tan.

'I'm sure you could do with a rest,' she said impulsively. 'I suppose you worked non-stop as usual?'

'It wasn't exactly a vacation,' he agreed briefly, 'though *you* look as if you've had one. Especially today. You're glowing.'

'Am I?' Julia moistened her lips. 'As a matter of fact, I . . . I have something important to tell you.'

'I have something important to say too. And it might be best if I spoke first. It could save you the embarrassment of having to tell me whatever it is you intended.'

'What makes you believe I'd be embarrassed?'

'I think I know you well enough,' he said quietly, and moved across to the fireplace. Idly he shifted a small jade figure on the mantelshelf, but she could tell it was a nervous gesture, something he was not aware of doing.

'Why don't you talk to me later?' she said huskily, 'after you've had a rest?'

He spun round. 'Because I won't be able to rest until I've spoken to you. What I have to say should have been said a long time ago, and I was a selfish swine to have waited so long.' He flung out his hands. 'You know what I am trying to say, don't you, Julia?'

'I'm not sure,' she whispered.

'I'm willing to give you your freedom,' he said. 'You won't need to beg me for it again.'

Julia felt the colour draining from her face, like sand from an hourglass. She wanted to speak but could not move her tongue.

'Don't look like that,' he said abruptly.

'Like—like what?'

'Unbelieving.' He fidgeted and looked down at the floor. 'You were right, Julia, and I was arrogantly wrong. Our marriage won't work. I've tried, and I'm sure you have, too, but I can't go on with it any longer.'

'I see.'

And Julia did—all too clearly. Adam no longer wanted to pretend he had a happy marriage, and this meant he had finally capitulated to Erica. Yet he had put up a terrific fight, making love to her night after night in the hope that it would help him forget the one woman he wanted above all others. Julia stifled a sigh. She should have guessed what was happening to him when he stopped coming to her. Admitting defeat, she silently went to the door.

'I'll pack my things,' she said quietly.

'There's no need for you to rush away.' His voice was husky. 'We can be civilised about the whole thing.'

'Oh, sure,' she said sarcastically. 'By all means let's be civilised.'

'I was referring to the way we end our marriage. It was never real, anyway,' he said heavily, and as she spun round and he saw her expression, his mouth narrowed. 'I'm not forgetting the way I behaved, Julia. I know I should never have touched you, but . . .' his voice was so low it was almost inaudible, 'but I thought that if . . . anyway, I was wrong. I now know one can never force love.'

'I agree,' she said dully, and turned again to the door.

'You won't be able to get an annulment,' he said behind

her. 'You realise that, don't you?'

She almost laughed aloud. As if she could ever forget it! Hysteria rose in her, but she clenched her hands and fought it down. She must never let him know about the baby. He wanted to be free of her and she would see that he was. Never would she use her pregnancy as a lever to keep him by her side.

'I'll try to move things as quickly as I can,' Adam went on. 'Would you like me to talk to Roy?'

Julia spun round again at this. 'What for? To explain why we can't get an annulment?'

Adam's face was as immovable as a mask, though his eyes glittered strangely. 'If it will make things easier for you, I'll tell him you were never willingly my wife. That I had to force you.'

She stared at him. 'You would admit that?'

'Yes. If it will ensure your happiness.'

It took Julia a moment to absorb the full meaning of what he had said. Then she gave a bitter smile. 'I don't think I need you to explain anything to Roy. He knows me well enough to realise I only lived with you under duress.' Flags of red stained Adam's cheeks and she knew her words had wounded him. But she wasn't finished yet either. There was one more salvo she had to fire. 'If you'd like me to tell Erica I forced myself on *you*,' she continued brightly, 'I'm only too happy to oblige.'

'I doubt if it would matter to Erica one way or the other,' he said curtly.

'You mean as long as she's the victor, she's willing to forget the past?'

Adam half turned away, giving Julia a view of his profile: the thick dark hair waving straight back from the high forehead, the firm, straight line of his nose and the narrow but well-shaped mouth, at this moment set in a rigid line.

'How long will we actually have to wait for a divorce?' Julia forced herself to ask.

'Two years. But with extenuating circumstances it may be less . . . I'll look into it and let you know.'

'It makes no difference to me,' she shrugged. 'And it won't matter to you either, will it? Erica will still have to wait until she's followed her late husband's wishes.'

'Yes.'

It was a clipped sound, as though forced from him, and it was more than Julia could bear. Her control snapped and anger exploded.

'You're crazy if you think you'll be happy with a woman like that! She doesn't love you, Adam. She's incapable of loving anyone except herself.'

'I don't comment on the way you intend running *your* life,' Adam glared, his own anger rising to meet hers. 'And I'll thank you to leave mine alone!'

'Gladly,' she flung at him. 'You're a fool—a blind, stupid fool!'

'I certainly *have* been,' he agreed bleakly. 'But not any more.'

He swung away from her and looked out of the window, his stance making it plain that the discussion was at an end.

For an instant, Julia watched him, then with a shiver she ran from the room.

But her bedroom was no haven, for it was filled with memories of Adam, and she knew she would have no peace until she had left this house and put behind her all her cherished plans for making it a home. Thank God she had not told Adam about the baby. But what would he have said if she had? And wasn't there a moral obligation for her to tell him? After all, it was his child, and even when they were divorced he would still have parental rights.

It was strange to think of Adam as a father, and it made Julia overwhelmingly conscious of the life within her. Would it be a boy or girl? she wondered, but knew it did not matter either way. The most important thing was that it would require Adam's love as much as her own. Wrenching open the door, she rushed down the stairs.

'Adam!' she cried as she ran towards the drawing room. 'Adam, I've got to talk to you.'

But the room was empty and his briefcase, which she had noticed on the settee, was gone. She ran back into the hall and was halfway up the stairs to his room when Emilio came through from the kitchen, waving an envelope at her.

'What is it?' she asked breathlessly.

'Mr Lester has gone out, madam, and he asked me to give you this letter.'

Julia waited as Emilio came up the stairs and handed her an envelope, though she did not open it until she was in the privacy of her room. It was a short note—the first one Adam had written to her since their marriage—and it was ironic it should be a goodbye letter.

'I'm staying at my club,' he began without preamble. 'Only for tonight, though, as I'm going to New York in the morning. I'll be away several weeks, which should give you ample time to make arrangements to leave. You'll still receive your allowance each quarter, and I would like you to use it. After the way I behaved to you it's the very least I can do. Believe me, Julia, I'm bitterly sorry for the way things turned out. I had hoped ...' These last three words were crossed out and he began a new paragraph.

'Please don't think of looking for another job—at least not yet. You've been through a rotten time and I think you should take yourself off somewhere for a decent holiday. Unless of course you decide to move in with Roy right away.'

Julia's hand clutched at the letter. Did Adam honestly believe she could go back to Roy, or was he making himself think it in order to lessen his guilt for breaking his side of their bargain? Well, there was one thing she had

learned for certain. One could never bargain when it came
to love. She let the letter drop on to the dressing table.
She couldn't tell Adam about the baby until he returned
from America, and by that time she might have decided
not to do so anyway. Perhaps it was better for a child to
have no father than a reluctant one; and the thought of
sharing her baby with Adam—once he was living with
Erica—was more than she could tolerate. She sat down in
front of the dressing table. 'You're glowing,' Adam had
said, implying that her meeting with Roy was the reason.

Poor, foolish Adam. If he only knew the truth!

CHAPTER TWELVE

THE prospect of living in a furnished flat again was so depressing that Julia could not bring herself to do anything about finding one, and for the next two days she mooned about the house like a zombie, unable to think clearly about anything.

A call from Betty Burglass finally forced her out of her gloom.

'We thought you might be lonely with Adam away again,' Betty said brightly. 'I know it's short notice, but if you aren't doing anything this evening, Jack and I would love you to come over to dinner. There'll just be the three of us and we can have a cosy chat.'

Julia could think of no good reason for refusing, yet as she replaced the receiver she wished she had not accepted the invitation. It would look peculiar if she didn't talk about Adam, yet how would Betty and Jack react if she spoke of him affectionately tonight and they discovered next week that they had parted? The whole idea was so embarrassing she decided it was best to stay at home.

She reached for the phone, but then stopped. To plead a headache was so palpably a lie that she could not do it. Besides, Jack and Betty had always been kind to her and she was reluctant to offend them, so short of telling them the truth she had no option but to go and put on an act. Still, it would be for the last time.

Anxious to look her best, she took great pains with her appearance, and was delighted how easily blushers and tinted foundation could transform a wan face into a glowing one. Only her eyes remained dead: blue glass that masked her inner turmoil. A full-skirted dress in warm shades of pink and rose softened the too slender lines of her figure, its ruffled neckline hiding the hollows at the base of her neck.

Jack and Betty greeted her warmly and she was surprised how at home she felt with them. They lived in an elegant town house bordering Regent's Park, and she enjoyed the informal dinner which they had in the rustic kitchen on the lower ground floor. It was evidently the staff's night out, for Betty prepared the meal herself: grilling steaks on a built-in charcoal grill, cooking jacket potatoes in the microwave oven—six minutes and they were ready—and tossing a huge green salad in a cut glass bowl, its oil and garlic dressing filling the air with a delicious if pungent aroma.

Talk was inconsequential as they sat around the wood table, enjoying the food and the delicious Burgundy which Jack poured with a lavish hand. Gradually Julia found herself relaxing, and for the first time no longer felt as if she were putting on an act. At this moment she really did feel Adam's wife, and for some unexpected reason the happiness she had been pretending was all at once real. She knew it was a sensation that would not last, but for as long as it did she was going to enjoy it.

'We were hoping marriage would stop Adam from rushing round the world,' said Betty as she poured the coffee. 'But it doesn't seem to have made any difference. You should start putting your foot down, Julia.'

'And have it trodden on?'

'Adam wouldn't do that,' Jack intervened. 'You should have seen the way he was watching you the other night at dinner. He looked positively fatuous!'

Julia forced a laugh. 'Adam could never look fatuous.'

'Well, he did. I know it's surprising to discover someone's a romantic when you've always thought of them as being incisive and businesslike, but take it from me, Adam's as romantic as hell where you're concerned. His face melts each time he looks at you.'

Julia refused to believe they were discussing the man

she knew. Even when making love to her Adam had never shown any special tenderness. True, his touch had been gentle, and even at the height of passion he had never been wholly absorbed in his own feelings, but had slowed his pace to try and make her response match his own. The fact that she had forcibly restrained herself from responding had never stopped him from trying to make her do so, and he had never—apart from that first angry taking of her—put his own passion ahead of hers. Yet he had never murmured words of love, never given away any of his thoughts. Silently he had come to her bed and silently he had left it. Yet tonight she found herself wondering if, like her, he had been reluctant to show his true feelings. Much as she longed to think this, she dismissed the thought, anxious not to let herself be swayed by Jack's interpretation of Adam's reaction to her.

'You're looking very pensive, Julia,' Betty said softly. 'I suppose you were wishing you were with Adam?'

'I was *thinking* about him,' Julia admitted, 'but I wasn't wishing I was with him. When he's working he's so absorbed in what he's doing that he doesn't have time for any one.'

'He'd always have time for you,' Jack insisted. 'Once Adam has given his love, it's for life. That's why he played the field so long and so hard—because he was scared of commitment. Being his own man—having total independence—has always been extremely important to him.'

'I wouldn't call it independence,' Julia replied bluntly. 'It's more a determination not to let anyone know his innermost feelings. Even if he has any doubts about anything, he'd never want anyone to know it.'

'That's understandable when you think of his background,' Jack said. 'If I'd had his sort of childhood I'd probably be the same.'

'He told me his mother and father were teachers,' Julia remarked, 'and that he came from the Midlands. But other than that, I know very little about him.'

Once again Jack did not hide his surprise. 'I know Adam hates talking about his past, but I assumed he'd told *you* about it.'

'Well, he hasn't—beyond saying that his parents were always preoccupied with themselves and he was left on his own a lot.'

'And nothing more than that?'

'No. *Is* there more?'

Jack's expression indicated that there was a great deal more, but from the look he gave his wife, Julia sensed his reluctance to tell her. Normally she would have let the matter rest, but because of her state of mind, every little detail of Adam's life was important to her.

'Please tell me,' she begged. 'Adam puzzles me so much at times that if there's anything in his past which would help me to understand his present behaviour, I'd like to know it.'

Still Jack hesitated.

'*Please,*' Julia reiterated. 'I'm not just being idly curious. Sometimes Adam's so—so distant that . . .' Her voice trailed away, for she was fearful of disclosing more than she should. But she seemed to have said enough, for Jack nodded, as if giving himself permission to speak.

'Adam was adopted,' he said.

'*Adopted?*'

'That's right. The woman he called his mother was actually his aunt. She didn't want to look after him, but she and her husband became his guardians out of a sense of obligation. If you want to make Adam furious, just fling the word "duty" at him,' Jack added.

'What happened to his own parents?'

'Adam's mother ran off with a trapeze artist when she was eighteen, but as soon as she became pregnant, he left her. A month afterwards he was killed in a road accident, but Adam's mother remained with the circus—they were pretty wonderful to her during her pregnancy, I believe, and after Adam was born she worked as assistant to the

SECOND BEST WIFE   175

owner. Then when Adam was four, she decided to take him to see her parents—by that time they'd decided to forgive her—and she was still in Yorkshire with them when she contracted polio and died.'

Julia was astounded. 'It sounds like an episode from a soap opera!'

'I know. But in this case it's true. Adam's grandparents decided they were too old to look after him, so his aunt and uncle adopted him instead.'

'How do you know all this?'

'Because Adam and I grew up in the same town, and you know what small towns are like. In those days it was quite a scandal for a girl to run off the way Adam's mother did, and then when she had a child . . .' Jack shook his head. 'Adam's aunt was a mean-spirited woman: an ardent churchgoer but devoid of compassion, and she never let Adam forget what he was. His grandfather was even worse. He'd set his heart on going into local politics, and during one election campaign a rival threw up a lot of dirt about Adam's mother, and his grandfather didn't get elected. He always blamed Adam for it, so you see, from the time he was about five, your husband was pretty long on duty and pretty short on love.'

Julia began to understand Adam's need for position and his determination never to be pitied.

'Tell me more about him,' she pleaded. 'As much as you can remember.'

'Well . . . he was extremely bright and won a scholarship to the local grammar school and then to university. His aunt and uncle began to take more interest in him, but it didn't fool Adam. He knew it only stemmed from their belief that he might bring fame and fortune to the family.'

'Did Adam tell you all this?' Julia questioned.

'Not at the time,' Jack admitted, 'but many years later, when his aunt was seriously ill. He was very cut up about it, too. That's when he confided in me.'

'It's strange he should have cared for her,' Julia said.

'Adam's always been loyal to his family. Pride, I suppose,' Jack explained. 'He even continued to visit his grandfather—for whom he didn't have much love—right up until the old man died. His grandfather was extremely proud of him by then, though Adam always underplayed his own power and prestige when he visited him.'

'It's hard to believe Adam had such a difficult childhood,' Betty commented. 'He's always so rational and cool.'

'Only in the outside,' her husband said. 'Inside, he's a complex man with a great need for love and support.' He gave Julia a searching look. 'Don't tell him what I've told you, my dear. Leave him to confide in you in his own good time.'

Julia nodded, knowing how wise the advice was, and wishing she had learned of Adam's past before she had married him. It was easy to see him as a lonely boy, deprived of affection and knowing he was living with a family that did not want him. It was not surprising he had taken Erica's rejection of him so badly; nor was it hard to guess why he still hankered after her. Getting her back would prove that everyone who rejected him ended up by wanting him.

'Adam's a changed man since he married you,' Jack said into the silence. 'When I asked him a while back to go with me to a business dinner, he said he preferred to spend the evening with you. I nearly fell off my seat with shock. Business always used to be his top priority.'

'He looks different too,' Betty added. 'Jack isn't the only one to see it. He's less hard and edgy, and when he focusses on you his whole face softens.'

Though Julia longed to be convinced, the memory of her last meeting with Adam made this impossible. More than ever she saw why Erica was important to him, and knew she could never tell him about the baby. Because of his own childhood and the loneliness he had experienced at not having a father, he would feel obligated to stay with her in order to give their child a family life—even if it were a false one. Envisaging all that this would mean, she knew it was far better for her to put as much distance as possible between them. She would leave London and live in the country, using his generous allowance to make a home for herself and her child. With luck, he need never know about the baby, and would probably think—when she took every penny he offered her—that she was as mercenary as Erica. It was a wry thought and Julia's lips curved upwards, which Betty Burglass was quick to notice, for she smiled approvingly, convinced her husband's explanation of Adam's past had eased Julia's mind.

'Would you like to spend next weekend with us in the country?' Betty asked. 'Adam said something to Jack about buying a place, and there's a lovely house not far from us which you could see. It would be marvellous to have you as neighbours.'

'I'm not too sure about next weekend,' Julia murmured. 'I'll talk to Adam and see when he's due back.'

Julia found it a relief to return to Chester Street and drop the façade she had maintained all evening. Entering the hall, she relaxed immediately, overcome by a deep sense of homecoming. It was strange that now she was about to leave here, Adam's house should begin to feel like home.

Yet this could never be the case. She must pack and be away from here by the time he returned to England. But where should she go? Staying with a girl friend was out of the question, for there would be too much explaining to do. Perhaps she should move into a hotel far from London until she found something permanent. At least then she would be out of sight and contact with Adam. Eventually he might discover she had had a baby, but she was certain he would think it was Roy's.

Resentment against Adam flared briefly within her and then died. After all, it was unfair to blame him for what had happened. She had gone into this marriage with her eyes open, never believing she would end up falling in love with him, or that she would become pregnant. Adam had talked of having a family, and she had assumed that if and when they consummated their relationship, it would be a commitment on Adam's side as well as her own.

Well, he had shown her plainly that his sexual relationship with her had not committed him whatever, and that he was willing to discard her the instant it suited him—though he had cleverly pretended he was setting her free because he knew it was what *she* wanted. Julia sighed heavily, remembering how many times she had begged Adam to do just that, though subconsciously she had hoped that when he agreed to let her go, he would realise she meant something to him. Tears flowed down her cheeks, but they brought only temporary relief, and she dried her eyes and vowed not to cry again. In the difficult months ahead she would need all the strength she could muster.

Next morning she rang an estate agent in Mayfair who put her in touch with their subsidiary branch in Gloucester. A soft-spoken man—elderly, by his tone— assured her she should have no difficulty acquiring a two or three-bedroomed cottage with a small garden.

'Naturally it will be in the region of forty thousand pounds,' he added. 'Is that all right for you?'

'Yes,' said Julia, knowing Adam would foot the bill. 'But I want to move quickly, so please see what you can do.'

On his promise that he would contact her within a few days, Julia ended the call and wandered over to the open window. It would be nice to live away from London, though she was not sure if she would like it in the winter. Nor did she know how she would keep herself occupied. She would be busy enough while the baby was small, but after that? She put her hands to her head. What a situation to be in: expecting a man's child and at the same time making plans to leave him.

There was a sound behind her and Emilio came into the room. 'Will you be in for lunch, madam?' he asked.

'I don't think so,' Julia replied, deciding not to stay home and brood. 'But I should be back around four.'

For several hours she wandered around Knightsbridge and Hyde Park. But even here she could not escape painful thoughts as she saw happy mothers wheeling babies in prams or playing with toddlers on the grass. Yet perhaps some of these women also lived alone; after all, these days one-parent families were not unusual. At least she herself was lucky to have a rich man to support her.

Impulsively she hailed a taxi and asked to be taken to Fortnums. Buying something new was supposed to be good therapy for an unhappy woman, and since she was soon going to be a wealthy divorcee, she might as well spend some of Adam's money right now.

By the time she reached the store, her enthusiasm had waned, and she strolled aimlessly around the dress department, unwilling to buy anything. Suddenly she felt someone staring at her, and from the corner of her eye caught a glimpse of pale blonde hair. She stiffened and drew back behind a display of cashmere dresses, but it was too late to escape, for Erica was already bearing down on her.

'So we meet in our local village shop,' the woman said lightly. 'You must enjoy coming here, now that you're able to afford it.'

Julia felt no anger at the remark, only a sense of depression that Adam could love a woman of such mean spirit. She made to walk on, but to her dismay Erica kept pace with her.

'I suppose you're feeling very pleased with yourself that your gamble's paid off?' Erica went on.

At a loss to know what this meant, Julia did not answer.

'Not that I give a damn,' the other girl continued disdainfully. 'I wouldn't have been happy with him anyway. He was always far too intense for me.'

'Really?' Julia said offhandedly.

'You'll get tired of him in the end too, unless you don't mind playing the role of Lady Perfect—if you know what I mean.'

'I'm afraid I *don't* know what you mean,' Julia retorted, throwing discretion to the wind. 'Would you care to be more explicit?'

An ugly flush stained Erica's face. 'You do want your pound of flesh, don't you? Still, as I said a moment ago, you're more than welcome to Adam. If I had to choose all over again, I'd still opt for Kenneth's money.'

'You always did.'

'Not always,' Erica snapped. 'And don't look so innocently at me. You know damn well I told Adam I'd be willing to forgo Kenneth's money and marry him as soon as he was free of you. But the damn fool said no—luckily for me. If he hadn't, I might have been lumbered with a decision made simply when I was feeling in the mood for sex.'

Julia could not believe that Adam had turned Erica down. Yet the woman had no reason to lie; on the contrary, it was amazing she had made such an admission. Yet she had only done so because she believed Adam had already told Julia what had happened.

As calmly as she could, Julia tried to assess Adam's behaviour. There were so many reasons for it that she forced herself not to think of any of them, determined that this she would ask him to tell her himself, and make no attempt to guess, for should she guess wrong, she would be opening the door on continuing anguish. The fact that Adam had come to his senses over Erica didn't mean he had fallen in love with his wife. If he had, he would never have suggested they dissolve their marriage.

Unless he genuinely believed she wanted to marry Roy?

Again there was only one way to find out: throw pride to the wind and ask him.

Disregarding Erica, who was still walking abreast of her, Julia spun round in the direction of the lift.

'What's wrong?' Erica asked.

'Nothing. Everything may be very right.'

'I don't understand you.'

'You never did,' said Julia, and sped away before Erica could say another word.

Never had a taxi travelled as slowly as the one that took Julia back home. Arriving there, she went straight to Adam's bedroom, as if to bring him closer to her. But it only made her feel lonelier, and she wished she had the courage to fly to New York and speak to him. Yet fear held her back. If he loved her, why hadn't he said so? How could he have held her in his arms and kissed her without showing his true feelings? Yet she had done exactly the same, so why should she be surprised by Adam's behaviour?

For the rest of the day she could think of nothing except Erica's dramatic revelation, and in bed that night she was both too excited and too fearful to sleep. Common sense still warned her not to set too much store by what she had learned, without first having it confirmed by Adam.

It was all she could do not to telephone him in New York to find out when he was coming home, but as a compromise she called the office and spoke to Susan, managing to discover he was due back at the weekend. Never had days passed so slowly and, when Saturday came and went without his arriving, she was overwhelmed by disappointment.

She slept badly on Saturday night and was up early next day. She mooned around unhappily and left her breakfast and lunch almost untouched. In the afternoon she changed into her prettiest dress. Her eyes were large and luminous and the colour came and went in her face. She was brushing her hair when she heard a car door slam. Running to the window, she peered down into the street and saw Adam's dark head. Now that the long-awaited moment had come, she was petrified to leave the safety of her room, and for several moments remained motionless, her mind in a whirl.

There was a tap on her door, and shakily she called, 'Come in.'

Adam did so. He seemed taller and darker than she remembered, but that was because he was thinner, and had deep shadows beneath his eyes.

'I didn't think I'd still find you here,' he said jerkily.

'Was I supposed to leave immediately?'

'I assumed you'd prefer it.'

'We're not parting as enemies,' she returned. 'That's what you yourself said.'

'I know.' He clenched his jaw as though trying to control the muscles of his face. 'When will you be going?'

'I'm not sure. That depends on you.'

'What do you mean?'

Julia's legs suddenly went weak, and she sat down on the dressing table stool.

'I'm willing to stay with you, Adam,' she said, looking at the wall behind him. 'That is, if you want me.'

There was a long silence and Julia could not bear to look at him, afraid of seeing rejection on his face.

'Why this sudden change of heart?' he asked slowly.

'It isn't a change of heart. You're the one who expected me to go, remember?'

'What makes you think I've changed my mind? The situation between us is still the same. You don't need to sacrifice yourself on my account, Julia.'

'I don't see it as a sacrifice.'

'Well, I do. And it isn't necessary. I don't need your presence here to bolster my pride.' He moved a step towards her and then stopped. 'If you want the truth, you might as well know that I no longer care what other people think of me. The few friends I have will accept me as I am—warts and all—and if my enemies laugh at me, then let them. It's what *I* feel that matters.'

Julia studied Adam's face for some sign that he meant what he said. But he was still too much in control of himself to give anything away, and though his words depicted a great change of attitude, he looked as aloof and controlled as ever.

'Have you really changed?' she asked slowly.

He half turned away from her. 'Once you start loving someone else more than you love yourself, you find that . . .' He let his voice trail off.

'You find what?' Julia whispered.

He remained silent, and it was a moment before he replied. 'You find you want that other person's happiness more than your own. Suddenly your own ambitions become less important and your friends' opinions have no importance at all.'

'You've come a long way in a very short time,' Julia said, then taking a deep breath, added: 'You must love Erica very deeply to have changed so much.'

'Erica!' It was a strangled sound, and Adam spun round. 'Erica's the last person I——' He stopped, as though trying to control himself. 'I don't love Erica,' he stated. 'It's *you* I'm talking about. *You* I love. Your happiness means more to me than my own. That's why I want you to be free. When I saw you with Roy the other day, I knew I couldn't tie you to me any longer. I've done everything possible to make you love me, but I've failed.'

'You haven't,' she denied.

'Don't bother sparing my feelings, Julia. You have every right to hate me. I forced myself on you night after night, but never once did you respond to me. All I felt was your disgust—your hate.'

'Not hate,' she cried. 'Only anger and hurt that you should want to claim your rights when you didn't care about me.'

'Is that what you thought? Didn't you feel anything

when I held you in my arms? Damn it! I told you, but you refused to believe me. Had you no idea how much I *did* care?' With a gesture of despair he flung out his hands. 'I thought that if I made love to you—if you were physic-ally mine—you'd stop thinking of Roy. But you said nothing . . . gave nothing away.'

'We both put on an act,' she said.

Adam stared at her, then as her words sank in, colour suffused his face. 'Both?' he echoed. 'What are you trying to tell me?'

'That I love you. That from the moment Roy came back from Canada and I saw him again, I knew it was *you* I wanted. But I thought you still loved Erica, so I wasn't going to admit the way I felt.'

'Is that why you agreed to leave me?' Adam crossed the carpet and stopped within a foot of her. 'Why were you so quick to say you'd go?'

'Yes. I thought you wanted to be free. You actually said so.'

'I was lying. I didn't want you to have any guilt about leaving me.'

Julia gave a sudden laugh, husky and bordering on tears. 'What a couple of fools we've been!'

'Not fools,' he said, pulling her into his arms. 'Just two people who'd been hurt and were scared of being hurt again.'

Bodies close, they rested against each other. Julia felt Adam tremble and knew her nearness was arousing him. She undid his jacket and put her hands on his chest, feeling the warmth of his body through the fine silk of his shirt.

'I saw Erica today,' she murmured. 'She told me you'd turned her down and——'

'So that's why you started wondering who I was in love with?'

Julia nodded. 'I hoped it was me, but I was afraid to let myself believe it.' Her fingers undid the buttons on his shirt and then caressed his skin. 'Why did you stop coming to me—stop making love to me?' she whispered.

'Because I'd reached the point where I couldn't bear making love to a woman who didn't want me. I stayed away because I loved you too much—not too little.' He tilted her face and rained little kisses across her brow and down her cheeks to her mouth. 'Give me a week to settle a couple of important cases, and then we'll go away for a real honeymoon. We'll begin our marriage again and pretend the past few months never happened.'

'We won't be able to pretend for long,' Julia murmured, laughter trembling in her voice.

'Oh?' Gently he lifted her into her arms and carried her to the bed. 'Why not?'

She waited till he was lying close beside her before she answered him. 'Because I'm going to have your child, Adam. In about seven months' time.'

A look of total amazement crossed his face, to be followed by such blazing joy that Julia had no need to ask if he were pleased.

'Oh, darling,' he said huskily. 'My dearest beloved darling.' Leaning over her, he reverently pressed his lips to her brow. 'Then you knew about it when I said I wanted a divorce?'

'Yes. It was the very day I'd been to see the doctor. I'd come home to tell you the news—I was hoping it would help us start our marriage afresh—and then you said you wanted me to go.'

He groaned and caught her in such a fierce grip that she winced. 'You must have thought me the biggest swine alive,' he muttered. 'If only you'd given me a hint of what had happened!'

'I thought you'd guess.' She stroked his hair, enjoying the knowledge that she no longer had to hide her desire for him. 'You're a potent man, my darling, and once or twice you took me by surprise.'

Raising himself slightly, he peered into her eyes. 'Do you mind about the baby, Julia?'

'What a crazy question! Why should I?'

'I only meant—because it wasn't conceived with love.'

'But it *was*. I've loved you for months, my darling, and you've just admitted *you* felt the same. The only trouble was that neither of us said so.'

'It's a deficiency I intend making up for,' he said, his voice unexpectedly urgent. 'I love you with my life, Julia, and I'll spend my life showing you exactly how much.'

'Could you begin now?' she asked teasingly, twining her hands around his neck and pulling him down on top of her.

'With pleasure,' he said thickly. 'With infinite, wonderful pleasure.'

Conscience, scandal and desire.

A dynamic story of a woman whose integrity, both personal and professional, is compromised by the intrigue that surrounds her.

Against a background of corrupt Chinese government officials, the CIA and a high powered international art scandal, Lindsay Danner becomes the perfect pawn in a deadly game. Only ex-CIA hit man Catlin can ensure she succeeds... and lives.

Together they find a love which will unite them and overcome the impossible odds they face.

Available May. Price £3.50

W⬤RLDWIDE

Best Seller Romances

Next month's best loved romances

Mills & Boon Best Seller Romances are the love stories that have proved particularly popular with our readers. These are the titles to look out for next month.

SMOKESCREEN
Anne Mather

THE MAGIC OF HIS KISS
Jessica Steele

Buy them from your usual paperback stockist, or write to: Mills & Boon Reader Service, P.O. Box 236, Thornton Rd, Croydon, Surrey CR9 3RU, England. Readers in Southern Africa — write to: Independent Book Services Pty, Postbag X3010, Randburg, 2125, S. Africa.

Mills & Boon
the rose of romance

As a regular subscriber you'll enjoy

★ **FOUR WONDERFUL NEW BOOKS** – every two months, reserved at the printers and delivered direct to your door by Mills & Boon.

★ **NO COMMITMENT** – you are under no obligation and may cancel your subscription at any time.

★ **FREE POSTAGE AND PACKING** – unlike many other book clubs we pay all the extras.

★ **FREE REGULAR NEWSLETTER** – packed with exciting competitions, horoscopes, recipes, and handicrafts... plus information on top Mills & Boon authors.

★ **SPECIAL OFFERS** – specially selected books and offers, created exclusively for Reader Service subscribers.

★ **HELPFUL, FRIENDLY SERVICE** – from the ladies at Mills & Boon. You can call us any time on 01- 684 2141.

With personal service like this, and wonderful stories like the one you've just read, is it really any wonder that Mills & Boon is the most popular publisher of romantic fiction in the world?

This attractive white canvas tote bag, emblazoned with the Mills & Boon rose, is yours absolutely **FREE!**

Just fill in the coupon today and post to:
MILLS & BOON READER SERVICE, FREEPOST,
PO BOX 236, CROYDON, SURREY CR9 9EL.